All Systems Red

T0286703

ALSO BY MARTHA WELLS

BOOKS OF THE RAKSURA
The Cloud Roads
The Serpent Sea
The Siren Depths
The Edge of Worlds
The Harbors of the Sun (forthcoming)
Stories of the Raksura: Volume I (short fiction)
Stories of the Raksura: Volume II (short fiction)

THE FALL OF ILE-RIEN TRILOGY
The Wizard Hunters
The Ships of Air
The Gate of Gods

STANDALONE ILE-RIEN BOOKS
The Element of Fire
The Death of the Necromancer
Between Worlds: The Collected Ile-Rien and Cineth Stories

YOUNG ADULT NOVELS
Emilie and the Hollow World
Emilie and the Sky World
Blade Singer (with Aaron de Orive)

TIE-IN NOVELS
Stargate Atlantis: Reliquary
Stargate Atlantis: Entanglement
Star Wars: Razor's Edge

City of Bones
Wheel of the Infinite

ALL SYSTEMS RED

THE MURDERBOT DIARIES

MARTHA WELLS

A TOM DOHERTY ASSOCIATES BOOK
NEW YORK

ALL SYSTEMS RED

Copyright © 2017 by Martha Wells

Cover illustration by Jaime Jones
Cover design by Christine Foltzer

Edited by Lee Harris

A Tor.com Book
Published by Tom Doherty Associates
175 Fifth Avenue
New York, NY 10010

www.tor.com

Tor® is a registered trademark of
Macmillan Publishing Group, LLC.

ISBN 978-0-7653-9752-2 (ebook)
ISBN 978-0-7653-9753-9 (trade paperback)

First Edition: May 2017

16 18 20 19 17 15

All Systems Red

Chapter One

I COULD HAVE BECOME a mass murderer after I hacked my governor module, but then I realized I could access the combined feed of entertainment channels carried on the company satellites. It had been well over 35,000 hours or so since then, with still not much murdering, but probably, I don't know, a little under 35,000 hours of movies, serials, books, plays, and music consumed. As a heartless killing machine, I was a terrible failure.

I was also still doing my job, on a new contract, and hoping Dr. Volescu and Dr. Bharadwaj finished their survey soon so we could get back to the habitat and I could watch episode 397 of *Rise and Fall of Sanctuary Moon*.

I admit I was distracted. It was a boring contract so far and I was thinking about backburnering the status alert channel and trying to access music on the entertainment feed without HubSystem logging the extra activity. It was trickier to do it in the field than it was in the habitat.

This assessment zone was a barren stretch of coastal island, with low, flat hills rising and falling and thick greenish-black grass up to my ankles, not much in the way of flora or fauna, except a bunch of different-sized birdlike things and some puffy floaty things that were harmless as far as we knew. The coast was dotted with big bare craters, one of which Bharadwaj and Volescu were taking samples in. The planet had a ring, which from our current position dominated the horizon when you looked out to sea. I was looking at the sky and mentally poking at the feed when the bottom of the crater exploded.

I didn't bother to make a verbal emergency call. I sent the visual feed from my field camera to Dr. Mensah's, and jumped down into the crater. As I scrambled down the sandy slope, I could already hear Mensah over the emergency comm channel, yelling at someone to get the hopper in the air now. They were about ten kilos away, working on another part of the island, so there was no way they were going to get here in time to help.

Conflicting commands filled my feed but I didn't pay attention. Even if I hadn't borked my own governor module, the emergency feed took priority, and it was chaotic, too, with the automated HubSystem wanting data and trying to send me data I didn't need yet and Mensah sending me telemetry from the hopper. Which I also didn't need, but it was easier to ignore than HubSystem simultaneously demanding answers and trying to supply them.

In the middle of all that, I hit the bottom of the crater. I have small energy weapons built into both arms, but the one I went for was the big projectile weapon clamped to my back. The hostile that had just exploded up out of the ground had a really big mouth, so I felt I needed a really big gun.

I dragged Bharadwaj out of its mouth and shoved myself in there instead, and discharged my weapon down its throat and then up toward where I hoped the brain would be. I'm not sure if that all happened in that order; I'd have to replay my own field camera feed. All I knew was that I had Bharadwaj, and it didn't, and it had disappeared back down the tunnel.

She was unconscious and bleeding through her suit from massive wounds in her right leg and side. I clamped the weapon back into its harness so I could lift her with both arms. I had lost the armor on my left arm and a lot of the flesh underneath, but my nonorganic parts were still working. Another burst of commands from the governor module came through and I backburnered it without bothering to decode them. Bharadwaj, not having nonorganic parts and not as easily repaired as me, was definitely a priority here and I was mainly interested in what the MedSystem was trying to tell me on the emergency feed. But first I needed to get her out of the crater.

During all this, Volescu was huddled on the churned

up rock, losing his shit, not that I was unsympathetic. I was far less vulnerable in this situation than he was and I wasn't exactly having a great time either. I said, "Dr. Volescu, you need to come with me now."

He didn't respond. MedSystem was advising a tranq shot and *blah blah blah,* but I was clamping one arm on Dr. Bharadwaj's suit to keep her from bleeding out and supporting her head with the other, and despite everything I only have two hands. I told my helmet to retract so he could see my human face. If the hostile came back and bit me again, this would be a bad mistake, because I did need the organic parts of my head. I made my voice firm and warm and gentle, and said, "Dr. Volescu, it's gonna be fine, okay? But you need to get up and come help me get her out of here."

That did it. He shoved to his feet and staggered over to me, still shaking. I turned my good side toward him and said, "Grab my arm, okay? Hold on."

He managed to loop his arm around the crook of my elbow and I started up the crater towing him, holding Bharadwaj against my chest. Her breathing was rough and desperate and I couldn't get any info from her suit. Mine was torn across my chest so I upped the warmth on my body, hoping it would help. The feed was quiet now, Mensah having managed to use her leadership priority to mute everything but MedSystem and the hopper, and all

I could hear on the hopper feed was the others frantically shushing each other.

The footing on the side of the crater was lousy, soft sand and loose pebbles, but my legs weren't damaged and I got up to the top with both humans still alive. Volescu tried to collapse and I coaxed him away from the edge a few meters, just in case whatever was down there had a longer reach than it looked.

I didn't want to put Bharadwaj down because something in my abdomen was severely damaged and I wasn't sure I could pick her up again. I ran my field camera back a little and saw I had gotten stabbed with a tooth, or maybe a cilia. Did I mean a cilia or was that something else? They don't give murderbots decent education modules on anything except murdering, and even those are the cheap versions. I was looking it up in HubSystem's language center when the little hopper landed nearby. I let my helmet seal and go opaque as it settled on the grass.

We had two standard hoppers: a big one for emergencies and this little one for getting to the assessment locations. It had three compartments: one big hub in the middle for the human crew and two smaller ones to each side for cargo, supplies, and me. Mensah was at the controls. I started walking, slower than I normally would have because I didn't want to lose Volescu. As the ramp started to drop, Pin-Lee and Arada jumped out and I switched to voice comm to say, "Dr. Mensah, I can't let go of her suit."

It took her a second to realize what I meant. She said hurriedly, "That's all right, bring her up into the crew cabin."

Murderbots aren't allowed to ride with the humans and I had to have verbal permission to enter. With my cracked governor there was nothing to stop me, but not letting anybody, especially the people who held my contract, know that I was a free agent was kind of important. Like, not having my organic components destroyed and the rest of me cut up for parts important.

I carried Bharadwaj up the ramp into the cabin, where Overse and Ratthi were frantically unclipping seats to make room. They had their helmets off and their suit hoods pulled back, so I got to see their horrified expressions when they took in what was left of my upper body through my torn suit. I was glad I had sealed my helmet.

This is why I actually like riding with the cargo. Humans and augmented humans in close quarters with murderbots is too awkward. At least, it's awkward for this murderbot. I sat down on the deck with Bharadwaj in my lap while Pin-Lee and Arada dragged Volescu inside.

We left two pacs of field equipment and a couple of instruments behind, still sitting on the grass where Bharadwaj and Volescu had been working before they went down to the crater for samples. Normally I'd help carry them, but MedSystem, which was monitoring Bharadwaj through what was left of her suit, was pretty clear that letting go of her would be a bad idea. But no one mentioned the equipment. Leaving easily replaceable items behind may seem obvious in an emergency, but I had been on contracts where the clients would have told me to put the bleeding human down to go get the stuff.

On this contract, Dr. Ratthi jumped up and said, "I'll get the cases!"

I yelled, "No!" which I'm not supposed to do; I'm always supposed to speak respectfully to the clients, even when they're about to accidentally commit suicide. Hub-System could log it and it could trigger punishment through the governor module. If it wasn't hacked.

Fortunately, the rest of the humans yelled "No!" at the same time, and Pin-Lee added, "For fuck's sake, Ratthi!"

Ratthi said, "Oh, no time, of course. I'm sorry!" and hit the quick-close sequence on the hatch.

So we didn't lose our ramp when the hostile came up under it, big mouth full of teeth or cilia or whatever chewing right through the ground. There was a great view of it on the hopper's cameras, which its system helpfully sent straight to everybody's feed. The humans screamed.

Mensah pushed us up into the air so fast and hard I nearly leaned over, and everybody who wasn't on the floor ended up there.

In the quiet afterward, as they gasped with relief, Pin-Lee said, "Ratthi, if you get yourself killed—"

"You'll be very cross with me, I know." Ratthi slid down the wall a little more and waved weakly at her.

"That's an order, Ratthi, don't get yourself killed," Mensah said from the pilot's seat. She sounded calm, but I have security priority, and I could see her racing heart-beat through MedSystem.

Arada pulled out the emergency medical kit so they could stop the bleeding and try to stabilize Bharadwaj. I tried to be as much like an appliance as possible, clamping the wounds where they told me to, using my failing body temperature to try to keep her warm, and keeping my head down so I couldn't see them staring at me.

```
performance reliability at 60% and dropping
```

Our habitat is a pretty standard model, seven interconnected domes set down on a relatively flat plain above a narrow river valley, with our power and recycling system connected on one side. We had an environmental system, but no air locks, as the planet's atmosphere was breathable, just not particularly good for humans for the long term. I don't know why, because it's one of those things I'm not contractually obligated to care about.

We picked the location because it's right in the middle of the assessment area, and while there are trees scattered through the plain, each one is fifteen or so meters tall, very skinny, with a single layer of spreading canopy, so it's hard for anything approaching to use them as cover. Of course, that didn't take into account anything approaching via tunnel.

We have security doors on the habitat for safety but HubSystem told me the main one was already open as the hopper landed. Dr. Gurathin had a lift gurney ready and guided it out to us. Overse and Arada had managed to get Bharadwaj stabilized, so I was able to put her down on it and follow the others into the habitat.

The humans headed for Medical and I stopped to send the little hopper commands to lock and seal itself, then I locked the outer doors. Through the security feed, I told the drones to widen our perimeter so I'd have more warning if something big came at us. I also set some monitors on the seismic sensors to alert me to anomalies just in case the hypothetical something big decided to tunnel in.

After I secured the habitat, I went back to what was

called the security ready room, which was where weapons, ammo, perimeter alarms, drones, and all the other supplies pertaining to security were stored, including me. I shed what was left of the armor and on MedSystem's advice sprayed wound sealant all over my bad side. I wasn't dripping with blood, because my arteries and veins seal automatically, but it wasn't nice to look at. And it hurt, though the wound seal did numb it a little. I had already set an eight-hour security interdiction through HubSystem, so nobody could go outside without me, and then set myself as off-duty. I checked the main feed but no one was filing any objections to that.

I was freezing because my temperature controls had given out at some point on the way here, and the protective skin that went under my armor was in pieces. I had a couple of spares but pulling one on right now would not be practical, or easy. The only other clothing I had was a uniform I hadn't worn yet, and I didn't think I could get it on, either. (I hadn't needed the uniform because I hadn't been patrolling inside the habitat. Nobody had asked for that, because with only eight of them and all friends, it would be a stupid waste of resources, namely me.) I dug around one-handed in the storage case until I found the extra human-rated medical kit I'm allowed in case of emergencies, and opened it and got the survival blanket out. I wrapped up in it, then climbed into the plastic bed of my cubicle. I let the door seal as the white light flickered on.

It wasn't much warmer in there, but at least it was cozy. I connected myself to the resupply and repair leads, leaned back against the wall and shivered. MedSystem helpfully informed me that my performance reliability was now at 58 percent and dropping, which was not a surprise. I could definitely repair in eight hours, and probably mostly regrow my damaged organic components, but at 58 percent, I doubted I could get any analysis done in the meantime. So I set all the security feeds to alert me if anything tried to eat the habitat and started to call up the supply of media I'd downloaded from the entertainment feed. I hurt too much to pay attention to anything with a story, but the friendly noise would keep me company.

Then someone knocked on the cubicle door.

I stared at it and lost track of all my neatly arrayed inputs. Like an idiot, I said, "Uh, yes?"

Dr. Mensah opened the door and peered in at me. I'm not good at guessing actual humans' ages, even with all the visual entertainment I watch. People in the shows don't usually look much like people in real life, at least not in the good shows. She had dark brown skin and lighter brown hair, cut very short, and I'm guessing she wasn't young or she wouldn't be in charge. She said, "Are you all right? I saw your status report."

"Uh." That was the point where I realized that I should have just not answered and pretended to be in stasis. I pulled the blanket around my chest, hoping she hadn't seen any of the missing chunks. Without the armor holding me together, it was much worse. "Fine."

So, I'm awkward with actual humans. It's not paranoia about my hacked governor module, and it's not them; it's me. I know I'm a horrifying murderbot, and they know it, and it makes both of us nervous, which makes me even more nervous. Also, if I'm not in the armor then it's because I'm wounded and one of my organic parts may fall off and plop on the floor at any moment and no one wants to see that.

"Fine?" She frowned. "The report said you lost 20 percent of your body mass."

"It'll grow back," I said. I know to an actual human I probably looked like I was dying. My injuries were the equivalent of a human losing a limb or two plus most of their blood volume.

"I know, but still." She eyed me for a long moment, so long I tapped the security feed for the mess, where the non-wounded members of the group were sitting around the table talking. They were discussing the possibility of more underground fauna and wishing they had intoxicants. That seemed pretty normal. She continued, "You were very good with Dr. Volescu. I don't think the others realized . . . They were very impressed."

"It's part of the emergency med instructions, calming victims." I tugged the blanket tighter so she didn't see anything awful. I could feel something lower down leaking.

"Yes, but the MedSystem was prioritizing Bharadwaj and didn't check Volescu's vital signs. It didn't take into account the shock of the event, and it expected him to be able to leave the scene on his own."

On the feed it was clear that the others had reviewed Volescu's field camera video. They were saying things like *I didn't even know it had a face.* I'd been in armor since we arrived, and I hadn't unsealed the helmet when I was around them. There was no specific reason. The only part of me they would have seen was my head, and it's standard, generic human. But they didn't want to talk to me and I definitely didn't want to talk to them; on duty it would distract me and off duty . . . I didn't want to talk to them. Mensah had seen me when she signed the rental contract. But she had barely looked at me and I had barely looked at her because again, murderbot + actual human = awkwardness. Keeping the armor on all the time cuts down on unnecessary interaction.

I said, "It's part of my job, not to listen to the System feeds when they . . . make mistakes." That's why you need constructs, SecUnits with organic components. But she should know that. Before she accepted delivery of me, she had logged about ten protests, trying to get out of having to have me. I didn't hold it against her. I wouldn't have wanted me either.

Seriously, I don't know why I didn't just say *you're welcome* and *please get out of my cubicle so I can sit here and leak in peace.*

"All right," she said, and looked at me for what objectively I knew was 2.4 seconds and subjectively about twenty excruciating minutes. "I'll see you in eight hours. If you need anything before then, please send me an alert on the feed." She stepped back and let the door slide closed.

It left me wondering what they were all marveling at so I called up the recording of the incident. Okay, wow. I had talked to Volescu all the way up the side of the crater. I had been mostly concerned with the hopper's trajectory and Bharadwaj not bleeding out and what might come out of that crater for a second try; I hadn't been listening to myself, basically. I had asked him if he had kids. It was boggling. Maybe I had been watching too much media. (He did have kids. He was in a four-way marriage and had seven, all back home with his partners.)

All my levels were too elevated now for a rest period, so I decided I might as well get some use out of it and look at the other recordings. Then I found something weird. There was an "abort" order in the HubSystem command feed, the one that controlled, or currently believed it controlled, my governor module. It had to be a glitch. It didn't matter, because when MedSystem has priority—

```
              performance reliability at 39%
      stasis initiated for emergency repair sequence
```

Chapter Two

WHEN I WOKE UP, I was mostly all there again, and up to 80 percent efficiency and climbing. I checked all the feeds immediately, in case the humans wanted to go out, but Mensah had extended the security interdict on the habitat for another four hours. Which was a relief, since it would give me time to get back up to the 98 percent range. But there was also a notice for me to report to her. That had never happened before. But maybe she wanted to go over the hazard info package and figure out why it hadn't warned us about the underground hostile. I was wondering a little about that myself.

Their group was called PreservationAux and it had bought an option on this planet's resources, and the survey trip was to see if it was worth bidding on a full share. Knowing about things on the planet that might eat them while they're trying to do whatever it is they're doing was kind of important.

I don't care much about who my clients are or what they're trying to accomplish. I knew this group was from a freehold planet but I hadn't bothered to look up the specifics. Freehold meant it had been terraformed and colonized but wasn't affiliated with any corporate confederations. Basically *freehold* generally meant *shitshow* so I hadn't been expecting much from them. But they were surprisingly easy to work for.

I cleaned all the stray fluids off my new skin, then climbed out of the cubicle. That was when I realized I hadn't put the pieces of my armor up and it was all over the floor, covered with my fluids and Bharadwaj's blood. No wonder Mensah had looked into the cubicle; she had probably thought I was dead in there. I put it all back into its slots in the reclaimer for repair.

I had an alternate set, but it was still packed into storage and it would take extra time to pull it out and do the diagnostics and the fitting. I hesitated over the uniform, but the security feed would have notified Mensah that I was awake, so I needed to get out there.

It was based on a standard research group's uniforms, and meant to be comfortable inside the habitat: knit gray pants, long-sleeved T-shirt, and a jacket, like the exercise clothes humans and augmented humans wore, plus soft shoes. I put it on, tugged the sleeves down over the gunports on my forearms, and went out into the habitat.

I went through two interior secure doors to the crew area, and found them in the main hub in a huddle around a console, looking at one of the hovering displays. They were all there except Bharadwaj, who was still in the infirmary, and Volescu, who was sitting in there with her. There were mugs and empty meal packets on some of the consoles. I'm not cleaning that up unless I'm given a direct order.

Mensah was busy so I stood and waited.

Ratthi glanced at me, and then did a startled double take. I had no idea how to react. This is why I prefer wearing the armor, even inside the habitat where it's unnecessary and can just get in the way. Human clients usually like to pretend I'm a robot and that's much easier in the armor. I let my eyes unfocus and pretended I was running a diagnostic on something.

Clearly bewildered, Ratthi said, "Who is this?"

They all turned to look at me. All but Mensah, who was sitting at the console with the interface pressed to her forehead. It was clear that even after seeing my face on Volescu's camera video, they didn't recognize me without the helmet. So then I had to look at them and say, "I'm your SecUnit."

They all looked startled and uncomfortable. Almost as uncomfortable as I did. I wished I'd waited to pull the spare armor out.

Part of it is, they didn't want me here. Not here in their hub, but here on the planet. One of the reasons the bond company requires it, besides slapping more expensive markups on their clients, is that I was recording all their conversations all the time, though I wasn't monitoring anything I didn't need to do a half-assed version of my job. But the company would access all those recordings and data mine them for anything they could sell. No, they don't tell people that. Yes, everyone does know it. No, there's nothing you can do about it.

After a subjective half hour and an objective 3.4 seconds, Dr. Mensah turned, saw me, and lowered the interface. She said, "We were checking the hazard report for this region to try to learn why that thing wasn't listed under hazardous fauna. Pin-Lee thinks the data has been altered. Can you examine the report for us?"

"Yes, Dr. Mensah." I could have done this in my cubicle and we could have all saved the embarrassment. Anyway, I picked up the feed she was watching from HubSystem and started to check the report.

It was basically a long list of pertinent info and warnings on the planet and specifically the area where our habitat was, with emphasis on weather, terrain, flora, fauna, air quality, mineral deposits, possible hazards related to any and all of those, with connections to subreports with more detailed information. Dr. Gurathin, the least talkative one, was an augmented human and had his own implanted interface. I could feel him poking around in the data, while the others, using the touch interfaces, were just distant ghosts. I had a lot more processing power than he did, though.

I thought they were being paranoid; even with the interfaces you actually have to read the words, preferably all the words. Sometimes non-augmented humans don't do that. Sometimes augmented humans don't do it either.

But as I checked the general warning section, I noticed something was odd about the formatting. A quick comparison with the other parts of the report told me that yeah, something had been removed, a connection to a subreport broken. "You're right," I said, distracted as I rifled through data storage looking for the missing piece. I couldn't find it; it wasn't just a broken connection, somebody had actually deleted the subreport. That was supposed to be impossible with this type of planetary survey package, but I guess it wasn't as impossible as all that. "Something's been deleted from the warnings and the section on fauna."

The reaction to that in general was pretty pissed off. There were some loud complaints from Pin-Lee and Overse and dramatic throwing-hands-in-the-air from Ratthi. But, like I said, they were all friends and a lot less restrained with each other than my last set of contractual obligations. It was why, if I forced myself to admit it, I had actually been enjoying this contract, up until something tried to eat me and Bharadwaj.

SecSystem records everything, even inside the sleeping cabins, and I see everything. That's why it's easier to pretend I'm a robot. Overse and Arada were a couple, but from the way they acted they'd always been one, and they were best friends with Ratthi. Ratthi had an unrequited thing for Pin-Lee, but didn't act stupid about it. Pin-Lee was exasperated a lot, and tossed things around when the others weren't there, but it wasn't about Ratthi. I thought that being under the company's eye affected her more than the others. Volescu admired Mensah to the point where he might have a crush on her. Pin-Lee did, too, but she and Bharadwaj flirted occasionally in an old comfortable way that suggested it had been going on for a long time. Gurathin was the only loner, but he seemed to like being with the others. He had a small, quiet smile, and they all seemed to like him.

It was a low-stress group, they didn't argue much or antagonize each other for fun, and were fairly restful to be around, as long as they didn't try to talk or interact with me in any way.

Mid expression of frustration, Ratthi said, "So we have no way to know if that creature was an aberration or if they live at the bottom of all those craters?"

Arada, who was one of the biology specialists, said, "You know, I bet they do. If those big avians we saw on the scans land on those barrier islands frequently, that creature might be preying on them."

"It would explain what the craters are doing there," Mensah said more thoughtfully. "That would be one anomaly out of the way, at least."

"But who removed that subreport?" Pin-Lee said, which I agreed was the more important question here. She turned to me with one of those abrupt movements that I had taught myself not to react to. "Can the HubSystem be hacked?"

From the outside, I had no idea. It was as easy as breathing to do it from the inside, with the built-in interfaces in my own body. I had hacked it as soon as it had come online when we set up the habitat. I had to; if it monitored the governor module and my feed like it was supposed to, it could lead to a lot of awkward questions and me being stripped for parts. "As far as I know, it's possible," I said. "But it's more likely the report was damaged before you received the survey package."

Lowest bidder. Trust me on that one.

There were groans and general complaining about having to pay high prices for shitty equipment. (I don't take it personally.) Mensah said, "Gurathin, maybe you and Pin-Lee can figure out what happened." Most of my clients only know their specialties, and there's no reason to send a system specialist along on a survey trip. The company supplies all the systems and attachments (the medical equipment, the drones, me, etc.) and will maintain it as part of the overall package the clients purchase. But Pin-Lee seemed to be a gifted amateur at system interpretation, and Gurathin had an advantage with his internal interface. Mensah added, "In the meantime, does the DeltFall Group have the same survey package as we do?"

I checked. HubSystem thought it was likely, but we knew what its opinion was worth now. "Probably," I said. DeltFall was another survey group, like us, but they were on a continent on the opposite side of the planet. They were a bigger operation and had been dropped off by a different ship, so the humans hadn't met in person, but they talked over the comm occasionally. They weren't part of my contract and had their own SecUnits, the standard one per ten clients. We were supposed to be able to call on each other in emergencies, but being half a planet apart put a natural damper on that.

Mensah leaned back in her chair and steepled her fingers. "All right, this is what we'll do. I want you each to check the individual sections of the survey package for your specialties. Try to pinpoint any more missing information. When we have a partial list, I'll call DeltFall and see if they can send us the files."

That sounded like a great plan, in that it didn't involve me. I said, "Dr. Mensah, do you need me for anything else?"

She turned her chair to face me. "No, I'll call if we have any questions." I had worked for some contracts that would have kept me standing here the entire day and night cycle, just on the off chance they wanted me to do something and didn't want to bother using the feed to call me. Then she added, "You know, you can stay here in the crew area if you want. Would you like that?"

They all looked at me, most of them smiling. One disadvantage in wearing the armor is that I get used to opaquing the faceplate. I'm out of practice at controlling my expression. Right now I'm pretty sure it was somewhere in the region of stunned horror, or maybe appalled horror.

Mensah sat up, startled. She said hurriedly, "Or not, you know, whatever you like."

I said, "I need to check the perimeter," and managed to turn and leave the crew area in a totally normal way and not like I was fleeing from a bunch of giant hostiles.

———————

Back in the safety of the ready room, I leaned my head against the plastic-coated wall. Now they knew their murderbot didn't want to be around them any more than they wanted to be around it. I'd given a tiny piece of myself away.

That can't happen. I have too much to hide, and letting one piece go means the rest isn't as protected.

I shoved away from the wall and decided to actually do some work. The missing subreport made me a little cautious. Not that there were any directives about it. My education modules were such cheap crap; most of the useful things I knew about security I learned from the edutainment programming on the entertainment feeds. (That's another reason why they have to require these research groups and mining and biology and tech companies to rent one of us or they won't guarantee the bond; we're cheaply produced and we suck. Nobody would hire one of us for non-murdering purposes unless they had to.)

Once I got my extra suit skin and spare set of armor on, I walked the perimeter and compared the current readings of the terrain and the seismic scans to the one we took when we first arrived. There were some notes in the feed from Ratthi and Arada, that fauna like the one we were now calling Hostile One might have made all the anomalous craters in the survey area. But nothing had changed around the habitat.

I also checked to make sure both the big hopper and the little hopper had their full complement of emergency supplies. I packed them in there myself days ago, but I was mainly checking to make sure the humans hadn't done anything stupid with them since the last time I checked.

I did everything I could think of to do, then finally let myself go on standby while I caught up on my serials. I'd watched three episodes of *Sanctuary Moon* and was fast forwarding through a sex scene when Dr. Mensah sent me some images through the feed. (I don't have any gender or sex-related parts (if a construct has those you're a sexbot in a brothel, not a murderbot) so maybe that's why I find sex scenes boring. Though I think that even if I did have sex-related parts I would find them boring.) I took a look at the images in Mensah's message, then saved my place in the serial.

Confession time: I don't actually know where we are. We have, or are supposed to have, a complete satellite map of the planet in the survey package. That was how the humans decided where to do their assessments. I hadn't looked at the maps yet and I'd barely looked at the survey package. In my defense, we'd been here twenty-two planetary days and I hadn't had to do anything but stand around watching humans make scans or take samples of dirt, rocks, water, and leaves. The sense of urgency just wasn't there. Also, you may have noticed, I don't care.

So it was news to me that there were six missing sections from our map. Pin-Lee and Gurathin had found the discrepancies and Mensah wanted to know if I thought it was just the survey package being cheap and error-ridden or if I thought this was part of a hack. I appreciated the fact that we were communicating via the feed and that she wasn't making me actually speak to her on the comm. I was so appreciative I gave her my real opinion, that it probably was the fact that our survey package was a cheap piece of crap but the only way to know for certain was to go out and look at one of the missing sections and see if there was anything there besides more boring planet. I didn't phrase it exactly like that but that was what I meant.

She took her attention off the feed then, but I stayed alert, since I knew she tended to make her decisions fast and if I started a show again I'd just get interrupted. I did check the security-camera view of the hub so I could hear their conversation. They all wanted to check it out, and were just going back and forth on whether they should wait. They had just had a comm conversation with Delt-Fall on the other continent who had agreed to send copies of the missing survey package files. Some of the clients wanted to see if anything else was missing first, and others wanted to go now, and *blah, blah, blah.*

I knew how this was going to turn out.

It wasn't a long trip, not far outside the range of the other assessments they had been doing, but not knowing what they were flying into was definitely a red flag for security. In a smart world, I should go alone, but with the governor module I had to be within a hundred meters of at least one of the clients at all times, or it would fry me. They knew that, so volunteering to take a solo cross-continental trip might set off a few alarms.

So when Mensah opened the feed again to tell me they were going, I told her security protocols suggested that I should go, too.

Chapter Three

WE GOT READY to leave at the beginning of the day cycle, in the morning light, and the satellite weather report said it would be a good day for flying and scanning. I checked MedSystem and saw Bharadwaj was awake and talking.

It wasn't until I was helping to carry equipment to the little hopper that I realized they were going to make me ride in the crew cabin.

At least I was in the armor with my helmet opaqued. But when Mensah told me to get in the copilot's seat, it didn't turn out to be as bad as my first horrified realization. Arada and Pin-Lee didn't try to talk to me, and Ratthi actually looked away when I eased past him to get to the cockpit.

They were all so careful not to look at me or talk to me directly that as soon as we were in the air I did a quick spot check through HubSystem's records of their conversations. I had talked myself into believing that I hadn't actually lost it as much as I thought I had when Mensah had offered to let me hang out in the hub with the humans like I was an actual person or something.

The conversation they had immediately after that gave me a sinking sensation as I reviewed it. No, it had been worse than I thought. They had talked it over and all agreed not to "push me any further than I wanted to go" and they were all so nice and it was just excruciating. I was never taking off the helmet again. I can't do even the half-assed version of this stupid job if I have to talk to humans.

They were the first clients I'd had who hadn't had any previous experience with SecUnits, so maybe I could have expected this if I'd bothered to think about it. Letting them see me without the armor had been a huge mistake.

At least Mensah and Arada had overruled the ones who wanted to talk to me about it. Yes, talk to Murderbot about its feelings. The idea was so painful I dropped to 97 percent efficiency. I'd rather climb back into Hostile One's mouth.

I worried about it while they looked out the windows at the ring or watched their feeds of the hopper's scans of the new scenery, chatting on the comm with the others who were following our progress back in the habitat. I was distracted, but still caught the moment when the autopilot cut out.

It could have been a problem, except I was in the

copilot's seat and I could have taken over in time. But even if I hadn't been there, it would have turned out okay, because Mensah was flying and she never took her hands off the controls.

Even though the planetary craft autopilots aren't as sophisticated as a full bot-pilot system, some clients will still engage it and then walk into the back, or sleep. Mensah didn't and she made sure when the others flew they followed her rules. She just made some thoughtful grumpy noises and adjusted our course away from the mountain the failing autopilot would have slammed us into.

I had cycled out of horrified that they wanted to talk to me about my feelings into grateful that she had ordered them not to. As she restarted the autopilot, I pulled the log and sent it into the feed to show her it had cut out due to a HubSystem glitch. She swore under her breath and shook her head.

―――――――――

The missing map section wasn't that far outside our assessment range so we were there before I made a dent in the backlog of serials I'd saved to my internal storage. Mensah told the others, "We're coming up on it."

We had been traveling over heavy tropical forest,

where it flowed over deep valleys. Suddenly it dropped away into a plain, spotted with lakes and smaller copses of trees. There was a lot of bare rock, in low ridges and tumbled boulders. It was dark and glassy, like volcanic glass.

The cabin was quiet as everybody studied the scans. Arada was looking at the seismic data, bouncing it to the others back in the habitat through her feed.

"I don't see anything that would prevent the satellite from mapping this region," Pin-Lee said, her voice distant as she sorted through the data the hopper was pulling in. "No strange readings. It's weird."

"Unless this rock has some sort of stealth property that prevented the satellites from imaging it," Arada said. "The scanners are acting a little funny."

"Because the scanners suck corporation balls," Pin-Lee muttered.

"Should we land?" Mensah said. I realized she was asking me for a security assessment.

The scans were sort of working and marking some hazards, but they weren't any different hazards from what we'd run into before. I said, "We could. But we know there's at least one lifeform here that tunnels through rock."

Arada bounced a little in her seat, like she was impatient to get going. "I know we have to be cautious, but

I think we'd be safer if we knew whether these blank patches on the satellite scan were accidental or deliberate."

That was when I realized they weren't ignoring the possibility of sabotage. I should have realized it earlier, when Pin-Lee asked if HubSystem could be hacked. But humans had been looking at me and I had just wanted to get out of there.

Ratthi and Pin-Lee seconded her, and Mensah made her decision. "We'll land and take samples."

Over the comm from the habitat, Bharadwaj's voice said, "Please be careful." She still sounded shaky.

Mensah took us down gently, the hopper's pads touching the ground with hardly a thump. I was already up and at the hatch.

The humans had their suit helmets on so I opened the hatch and let the ramp drop. Close up the rocky patches still looked like glass, mostly black, but with different colors running into each other. This near to the ground the hopper's scan was able to confirm that seismic activity was null, but I walked out a little bit, as if giving anything out there a chance to attack me. If the humans see me actually doing my job, it helps keep suspicions from forming about faulty governor modules.

Mensah climbed down with Arada behind her. They moved around, taking more readings with their portable scanners. Then the others got the sample kit outs and started chipping off pieces of the rock glass, or glass rock, scooping up dirt and bits of plant matter. They were murmuring to each other a lot, and to the others back at the habitat. They were sending the data to the feed, but I wasn't paying attention.

It was an odd spot. Quiet compared to the other places we'd surveyed, with not much bird-thing noise and no sign of animal movement. Maybe the rocky patches kept them away. I walked out a little way, past a couple of the lakes, almost expecting to see something under the surface. Dead bodies, maybe. I'd seen plenty of those (and caused plenty of those) on past contracts, but this one had been dead-body-lacking, so far. It made for a nice change.

Mensah had set a survey perimeter, marking all the areas the aerial scan had flagged as hazardous or potentially hazardous. I checked on everybody again and saw Arada and Ratthi heading directly for one of the hazard markers. I expected them to stop at the perimeter, since they'd been pretty consistently cautious on the other assessments. I started moving in that direction anyway. Then they passed the perimeter. I started to run. I sent Mensah my field camera feed and used the voice comm to say, "Dr. Arada, Dr. Ratthi, please stop. You're past the perimeter and nearing a hazard marker."

"We are?" Ratthi sounded completely baffled.

Fortunately, they both stopped. By the time I got there they both had their maps up in my feed. "I don't understand what's wrong," Arada said, confused. "I don't see the hazard marker." She had tagged both their positions and on their maps they were well within the perimeter, heading toward a wetland area.

It took me a second to see what the problem was. Then I superimposed my map, the actual map, over theirs and sent that to Mensah. "Shit," she said over the comm. "Ratthi, Arada, your map's wrong. How did that happen?"

"It's a glitch," Ratthi said. He grimaced, studying the displays in his feed. "It's wiped out all the markers on this side."

So that was how I spent the rest of the morning, shooing humans away from hazard markers they couldn't see, while Pin-Lee cursed a lot and tried to get the mapping scanner to work. "I'm beginning to think these missing sections are just a mapping error," Ratthi said at one point, panting. He had walked into what they called a hot mud pit and I'd had to pull him out. We were both covered with acidic mud to the waist.

"You think?" Pin-Lee answered tiredly.

When Mensah told us to head back to the hopper, it was a relief all around.

———————

We got back to the habitat with no problems, which felt like it was starting to become an unusual occurrence. The humans went to analyze their data, and I went to hide in the ready room, check the security feeds, and then lie in my cubicle and watch media for a while.

I'd just done another perimeter walk and checked the drones, when the feed informed me that HubSystem had updates from the satellite and there was a package for me. I have a trick where I make HubSystem think I received it and then just put it in external storage. I don't do automated package updates anymore, now that I don't have to. When I felt like it, presumably sometime before it was time to leave the planet, I'd go through the update and apply the parts I wanted and delete the rest.

It was a typical, boring day, in other words. If Bharadwaj wasn't still recuperating in Medical, you could almost forget what had happened. But at the end of the day cycle, Dr. Mensah called me again and said, "I think we have a problem. We can't contact DeltFall Group."

———————

I went to the crew hub where Mensah and all the others were. They had pulled up the maps and scans of where we were versus where DeltFall was, and the curve of the planet hung glittering in the air in the big display. When I got there, Mensah was saying, "I've checked the big hopper's specs and we can make it there and back without a recharge."

I had my helmet plate opaqued, so I could wince a lot without any of them knowing.

"You don't think they'll let us recharge at their habitat?" Arada asked, then looked around when the others stared at her. "What?" she demanded.

Overse put an arm around her and squeezed her shoulder. "If they aren't answering our calls, they might be hurt, or their habitat is damaged," she said. As a couple, they were always so nice to each other. The whole group had been remarkably drama-free so far, which I appreciated. The last few contracts had been like being an involuntary bystander in one of the entertainment feed's multi-partner relationship serials except I'd hated the whole cast.

Mensah nodded. "That's my concern, especially if their survey package was missing potential hazard information the way ours is."

Arada looked like it was just occurring to her that everybody over at DeltFall might be dead.

Ratthi said, "The thing that worries me is that their emergency beacon didn't launch. If the habitat was breached, or if there was a medical emergency they couldn't handle, their HubSystem should have triggered the beacon automatically."

Each survey team has its own beacon, set up a safe distance from the habitat. It would launch into a low orbit and send a pulse toward the wormhole, which would get zapped or whatever happened in the wormhole and the company network would get it, and the pickup transport would be sent now instead of waiting until the end of project date. That was how it was supposed to work, anyway. Usually.

Mensah's expression said she was worried. She looked at me. "What do you think?"

It took me two seconds to realize she was talking to me. Fortunately, since it seemed like we were really doing this, I had actually been paying attention and didn't need to play the conversation back. I said, "They have three contracted SecUnits but if their habitat was hit by a hostile as big or bigger than Hostile One, their comm equipment could have been damaged."

Pin-Lee was calling up specs for the beacons. "Aren't the emergency beacons designed to trigger even if the rest of the comm equipment is destroyed?"

The other good thing about my hacked governor module is that I could ignore the governor's instructions to defend the stupid company. "They're supposed to be able to, but equipment failures aren't unknown."

There was a moment where they all thought about potential equipment failures in their habitat, maybe including the big hopper which they were about to fly out of range of the little hopper, so if something happened to it they were walking back. And swimming back, since that was an ocean-sized body of water between the two points on the map. Or drown; I guess they could just drown. If you were wondering why I was wincing earlier, this would be the reason.

The trip to the map's black-out region had been a little out of our assessment parameters, but this was going to be an overnight trip, even if all they did was get there, see a bunch of dead people, turn around and go back.

Then Gurathin said, "What about your systems?"

I didn't turn my helmet toward him because that can be intimidating and it's especially important for me to resist that urge. "I carefully monitor my own systems." What else did he think I was going to say? It didn't matter; I'm not refundable.

Volescu cleared his throat. "So we should prepare for a rescue mission." He looked okay, but MedSystem's feed was still reporting some indicators of distress. Bharadwaj was stable but not allowed to get out of Medical yet. He continued, "I've pulled some instructions from the hopper's info package."

Yes, instructions. They're academics, surveyors, researchers, not action-hero explorers from the serials I liked because they were unrealistic and not depressing and sordid like reality. I said, "Dr. Mensah, I think I should go along."

I could see her notes in the feed so I knew she meant for me to stay here and watch the habitat and guard everybody who wasn't going. She was taking Pin-Lee, because she had past experience in habitat and shelter construction; Ratthi, who was a biologist; and Overse, who was certified as a field medic.

Mensah hesitated, thinking about it, and I could tell she was debating protecting the habitat and the group staying behind with the possibility of whatever had hit DeltFall still being there. She took a breath and I knew she was going to tell me to stay here. And I just thought, *That's a bad idea.* I couldn't explain to myself why. It was one of those impulses that comes from my organic parts that the governor is supposed to squash. I said, "As the only one here with experience in these situations, I'm your best resource."

Gurathin said, "What situations?"

Ratthi gave him a bemused look. "This situation. The unknown. Strange threats. Monsters exploding out of the ground."

I was glad I wasn't the only one who thought it was a

dumb question. Gurathin wasn't as talkative as the others, so I didn't have much of a sense of his personality. He was the only augmented human in the group, so maybe he felt like an outsider, or something, even though the others clearly liked him. I clarified, "Situations where personnel might be injured due to attack by planetary hazards."

Arada came in on my side. "I agree. I think you should take SecUnit. You don't know what's out there."

Mensah was still undecided. "Depending on what we find, we may be gone as long as two or three days."

Arada waved a hand, indicating the habitat. "Nothing's bothered us here so far."

That was probably what DeltFall had thought, right before they got eaten or torn to pieces or whatever. But Volescu said, "I admit it would make me feel better about it." From Medical, Bharadwaj tapped into the feed to add her vote for me. Gurathin was the only one staying behind who didn't say anything.

Mensah nodded firmly. "All right then, it's decided. Now let's get moving."

———

So I prepped the big hopper to go to the other side of the planet. (And yes, I had to pull up the instructions.)

I checked it over as much as I could, remembering how the autopilot had cut out suddenly in the little hopper. But we hadn't used the big hopper since Mensah had taken it up to check it out when we arrived. (You had to check everything out and log any problems immediately when you took delivery or the company wasn't liable.) But everything looked okay, or at least matched what the specs said it was supposed to match. It was only there for emergencies and if this thing with DeltFall hadn't happened, we would probably never have touched it until it was time to lift it onto our pickup transport.

Mensah came to do her own check of the hopper, and told me to pack some extra emergency supplies for the DeltFall staff. I did it, and I hoped for the humans' sake we would need them. I thought it was likely that the only supplies we would need for DeltFall was the postmortem kind, but you may have noticed that when I do manage to care, I'm a pessimist.

When everything was ready, Overse, Ratthi, and Pin-Lee climbed in, and I stood hopefully by the cargo pod. Mensah pointed at the cabin. I winced behind my opaque faceplate and climbed in.

Chapter Four

WE FLEW THROUGH THE NIGHT, the humans taking scans and discussing the new terrain past our assessment range. It was especially interesting for them to see what was there, now that we knew our map wasn't exactly reliable.

Mensah gave everybody watch shifts, including me. This was new, but not unwelcome, as it meant I had blocks of time where I wasn't supposed to be paying attention and didn't have to fake it. Mensah, Pin-Lee, and Overse were all taking turns as pilot and copilot, so I didn't have to worry so much about the autopilot trying to kill us, and I could go on standby and watch my stored supply of serials.

We'd been in the air awhile, and Mensah was piloting with Pin-Lee in the copilot's seat, when Ratthi turned in his seat to face me and said, "We heard—we were given to understand, that Imitative Human Bot Units are . . . partially constructed from cloned material."

Warily, I stopped the show I was watching. I didn't like where this might go. All of that information is in the common knowledge database, plus in the brochure the company provides with the specifics of the types of units they use. Which he knew, being a scientist and whatever. And he wasn't the kind of human who asked about things when he could look them up himself through a feed. "That's true," I said, very careful to make my voice sound just as neutral as always.

Ratthi's expression was troubled. "But surely … It's clear you have feelings—"

I flinched. I couldn't help it.

Overse had been working in the feed, analyzing data from the assessments. She looked up, frowning. "Ratthi, what are you doing?"

Ratthi shifted guiltily. "I know Mensah asked us not to, but—" He waved a hand. "You saw it."

Overse pulled her interface off. "You're upsetting it," she said, teeth gritted.

"That's my point!" He gestured in frustration. "The practice is disgusting, it's horrible, it's slavery. This is no more a machine than Gurathin is—"

Exasperated, Overse said, "And you don't think it knows that?"

I'm supposed to let the clients do and say whatever they want to me and with an intact governor module I wouldn't have a choice. I'm also not supposed to snitch on clients to anybody except the company, but it was either that or jump out the hatch. I sent the conversation into the feed tagged for Mensah.

From the cockpit, she shouted, "Ratthi! We talked about this!"

I slid out of the seat and went to the back of the hopper, as far away as I could get, facing the supply lockers and the head. It was a mistake; it wasn't a normal thing for a SecUnit with an intact governor module to do, but they didn't notice.

"I'll apologize," Ratthi was saying.

"No, just leave it alone," Mensah told him.

"That would just make it worse," Overse added.

I stood there until they all calmed down and got quiet again, then slid into a seat in the back, and resumed the serial I'd been watching.

It was the middle of the night when I felt the feed drop out.

I hadn't been using it, but I had the SecSystem feeds from the drones and the interior cameras backburnered and was accessing them occasionally to make sure everything was okay. The humans left behind in the habitat were more active than they usually were at this time, probably anxious about what we were going to find at

DeltFall. I was hearing Arada walk around occasionally, though Volescu was snoring off and on in his bunk. Bharadwaj had been able to move back to her own quarters, but was restless and going over her field notes through the feed. Gurathin was in the hub doing something on his personal system. I wondered what he was doing and had just started to carefully poke around through HubSystem to find out. When the feed dropped it was like someone slapped the organic part of my brain.

I sat up and said, "The satellite went down."

The others, except for Pin-Lee who was piloting, all grabbed for their interfaces. I saw their expressions when they felt the silence. Mensah pushed out of her seat and came to the back. "Are you sure it was the satellite?"

"I'm sure," I told her. "I'm pinging it and there's no response."

We still had our local feed, running on the hopper's system, so we could communicate through it as well as the comm and share data with each other. We just didn't have nearly as much data as we'd have had if we were still attached to HubSystem. We were far enough away that we needed the comm satellite as a relay. Ratthi switched his interface to the hopper's feed and started checking the scans. There was nothing on them except empty sky; I had them backburnered but I'd set them to notify me if they encountered anything like an energy reading or a large life sign. He said, "I just felt a chill. Did anyone else feel a chill?"

"A little," Overse admitted. "It's a weird coincidence, isn't it?"

"The damn satellite's had periodic outages since we got here," Pin-Lee pointed out from the cockpit. "We just don't normally need it for comms." She was right. I was supposed to check their personal logs periodically in case they were plotting to defraud the company or murder each other or something, and the last time I'd looked at Pin-Lee's she had been tracking the satellite problems, trying to figure out if there was a pattern. It was one of the many things I didn't care about because the entertainment feed was only updated occasionally, and I downloaded it for local storage.

Ratthi shook his head. "But this is the first time we've been far enough from the habitat to need it for comm contact. It just seems odd, and not in a good way."

Mensah looked around at them. "Does anyone want to turn back?"

I did, but I didn't get a vote. The others sat there for a quiet moment, then Overse said, "If it turns out the Delt-Fall group did need help, and we didn't go, how would we feel?"

"If there's a chance we can save lives, we have to take it," Pin-Lee agreed.

Ratthi sighed. "No, you're right. I'd feel terrible if anyone died because we were overcautious."

"We're agreed, then," Mensah said. "We'll keep going."

I would have preferred they be overcautious. I had had contracts before where the company's equipment glitched this badly, but there was just something about this that made me think it was more. But all I had was the feeling.

I had four hours to my next scheduled watch so I went into standby, and buried myself in the downloads I'd stored away.

———

It was dawn when we got there. DeltFall had established their camp in a wide valley surrounded by high mountains. A spiderweb of creek beds cut through the grass and stubby trees. They were a bigger operation than ours, with three linked habitats, and a shelter for surface vehicles, plus a landing area for two large hoppers, a cargo hauler, and three small hoppers. It was all company equipment though, per contract, and all subject to the same malfunctions as the crap they'd dumped on us.

There was no one outside, no movement. No sign of damage, no sign any hostile fauna had approached. The satellite was still dead, but Mensah had been trying to get the DeltFall habitat on the comm since we had come within range.

"Are they missing any transports?" Mensah asked.

Ratthi checked the record of what they were supposed to have which I'd copied from HubSystem before we left. "No, the hoppers are all there. Their ground vehicles are in that shelter, I think."

I had moved up to the front as we got closer. Standing behind the pilot's seat, I said, "Dr. Mensah, I recommend you land outside their perimeter." Through the local feed I sent her all the info I had, which was that their automated systems were responding to the pings the hopper was sending, but that was it. We weren't picking up their feed, which meant their HubSystem was in standby. There was nothing from their three SecUnits, not even pings.

Overse, in the copilot's seat, glanced up at me. "Why?"

I had to answer the question so I said, "Security protocol," which sounded good and didn't commit me to anything. No one outside, no one answering the comm. Unless they had all jumped in their surface vehicles and gone off on vacation, leaving their Hub and SecUnits shut down, they were dead. Pessimism confirmed.

But we couldn't be sure without looking. The hopper's scanners can't see inside the habitats because of the shielding that's really only there to protect proprietary data, so we couldn't get any life signs or energy readings.

This is why I didn't want to come. I've got four perfectly good humans here and I didn't want them to get killed by whatever took out DeltFall. It's not like I cared about them personally, but it would look bad on my record, and my record was already pretty terrible.

"We're just being cautious," Mensah said, answering Overse. She took the hopper down at the edge of the valley, on the far side of the streams.

I gave Mensah a few hints through the feed, that they should break out the handweapons in the survival gear, that Ratthi should stay behind inside the hopper with the hatch sealed and locked since he'd never done the weapon-training course, and that, most important, I should go first. They were quiet, subdued. Up until now, I think they had all been looking at this as probably a natural disaster, that they were going to be digging survivors out of a collapsed habitat, or helping fight off a herd of Hostile Ones.

This was something else.

Mensah gave the orders and we started forward, me in front, the humans a few steps behind. They were in their full suits with helmets, which gave some protection but had been meant for environmental hazards, not some other heavily armed human (or angry malfunctioning rogue SecUnit) deliberately trying to kill them. I was more nervous than Ratthi, who was jittery on our comms, monitoring the scans, and basically telling us to be careful every other step.

I had my built-in energy weapons and the big projectile weapon I was cradling. I also had six drones, pulled from the hopper's supply and under my control through its feed. They were the small kind, barely a centimeter across; no weapons, just cameras. (They make some which aren't much bigger and have a small pulse weapon, but you have to get one of the upper-tier company packages mostly designed for much larger contracts.) I told the drones to get in the air and gave them a scouting pattern.

I did that because it seemed sensible, not because I knew what I was doing. I am not a combat murderbot, I'm Security. I keep things from attacking the clients and try to gently discourage the clients from attacking each other. I was way out of my depth here, which was another reason I hadn't wanted the humans to come here.

We crossed the shallow streams, sending a group of water invertebrates scattering away from our boots. The trees were short and sparse enough that I had a good view of the camp from this angle. I couldn't detect any DeltFall security drones, by eye or with the scanners on my drones. Ratthi in the hopper wasn't picking up anything either. I really, really wished I could pinpoint the location of those three SecUnits, but I wasn't getting anything from them.

SecUnits aren't sentimental about each other. We aren't friends, the way the characters on the serials are, or the way my humans were. We can't trust each other, even if we work together. Even if you don't have clients who decide to entertain themselves by ordering their SecUnits to fight each other.

The scans read the perimeter sensors as dead and the drones weren't picking up any warning indicators. The DeltFall HubSystem was down, and without it, no one inside could access our feed or comms, theoretically. We crossed over and into the landing area for their hoppers. They were between us and the first habitat, the vehicle storage to one side. I was leading us in at an angle, trying to get a visual on the main habitat door, but I was also checking the ground. It was mostly bare of grass from all the foot traffic and hopper landings. From the weather report we'd gotten before the satellite quit, it had rained here last night, and the mud had hardened. No activity since then.

I passed that info to Mensah through the feed and she told the others. Keeping her voice low, Pin-Lee said, "So whatever happened, it wasn't long after we spoke to them on the comm."

"They couldn't have been attacked by someone,"

Overse whispered. There was no reason to whisper, but I understood the impulse. "There's no one else on this planet."

"There's not supposed to be anyone else on this planet," Ratthi said, darkly, over the comm from our hopper.

There were three SecUnits who were not me on this planet, and that was dangerous enough. I got my visual on the main habitat hatch and saw it was shut, no sign of anything forcing its way inside. The drones had circled the whole structure by now, and showed me the other entrances were the same. That was that. Hostile Fauna don't come to the door and ask to be let inside. I sent the images to Mensah's feed and said aloud, "Dr. Mensah, it would be better if I went ahead."

She hesitated, reviewing what I'd just sent her. I saw her shoulders tense. I think she had just come to the same conclusion I had. Or at least admitted to herself that it was the strongest possibility. She said, "All right. We'll wait here. Make sure we can monitor."

She'd said "we" and she wouldn't have said that if she didn't mean it, unlike some clients I'd had. I sent my field camera's feed to all four of them and started forward.

I called four of the drones back, leaving two to keep circling the perimeter. I checked the vehicle shed as I moved past it. It was open on one side, with some sealed lockers in the back for storage. All four of their surface vehicles were there, powered down, no sign of recent tracks, so I didn't go in. I wouldn't bother searching the small storage spaces until we got down to the looking-for-all-the-body-parts phase.

I walked up to the hatch of the first habitat. We didn't have an entry code, so I was expecting to have to blow the door, but when I tapped the button it slid open for me. I told Mensah through the feed that I wouldn't speak aloud on the comm anymore.

She tapped back an acknowledgment on the feed, and I heard her telling the others to get off my feed and my comm, that she was going to be the only one speaking to me so I wasn't distracted. Mensah underestimated my ability to ignore humans but I appreciated the thought. Ratthi whispered, "Be careful," and signed off.

I had the weapon up going in, through the suit locker area and into the first corridor. "No suits missing," Mensah said in my ear, watching the field camera. I sent my four drones ahead, maintaining an interior scouting pattern. This was a nicer habitat than ours, wider halls, newer. Also empty, silent, the smell of decaying flesh drifting through my helmet filters. I headed toward the hub, where their main crew area should be.

The lights were still on and air whispered through the vents, but I couldn't get into their SecSystem with their feed down. I missed my cameras.

At the door to the hub, I found their first SecUnit. It was sprawled on its back on the floor, the armor over its chest pierced by something that made a hole approximately ten centimeters wide and a little deeper. We're hard to kill, but that'll do it. I did a brief scan to make sure it was inert, then stepped over it and went through into the crew area.

There were eleven messily dead humans in the hub, sprawled on the floor, in chairs, the monitoring stations and projection surfaces behind them showing impact damage from projectile and energy weapon fire. I tapped the feed and asked Mensah to fall back to the hopper. She acknowledged me and I got confirmation from my outside drones that the humans were retreating.

I went out the opposite door to a corridor that led toward the mess hall, Medical, and cabins. The drones were telling me the layout was very similar to our habitat, except for the occasional dead person sprawled in the corridors. The weapon that had taken out the dead SecUnit wasn't in the hub, and it had died with its back to the door. The DeltFall humans had had some warning, enough to start getting up and heading for the other exits, but something else had come in from this direction and trapped them. I thought that SecUnit had been killed trying to protect the hub.

Which meant I was looking for the other two SecUnits.

Maybe these clients had been terrible and abusive, maybe they had deserved it. I didn't care. Nobody was touching my humans. To make sure of that I had to kill these two rogue Units. I could have pulled out at this point, sabotaged the hoppers, and got my humans out of there, leaving the rogue Units stuck on the other side of an ocean; that would have been the smart thing to do.

But I wanted to kill them.

One of my drones found two humans dead in the mess, no warning. They had been taking food pacs out of the heating cubby, getting the tables ready for a meal.

While I moved through the corridors and rooms, I was doing an image search against the hopper's equipment database. The dead unit had probably been killed by a mineral survey tool, like a pressure or sonic drill. We had one on the hopper, part of the standard equipment. You would have to get close to use it with enough force to pierce armor, maybe a little more than a meter.

Because you can't walk up to another murderbot with an armor-piercing projectile or energy weapon inside the habitat and not be looked at with suspicion. You can walk up to a fellow murderbot with a tool that a human might have asked you to get.

By the time I reached the other side of the structure,

the drones had cleared the first habitat. I stood in the hatchway at the top of the narrow corridor that led into the second. A human lay at the opposite end, half in and half out of the open hatch. To get into the next habitat, I'd have to step over her to push the door all the way open. I could tell already that something was wrong about the body position. I used the magnification on the field camera to get a closer view of the skin on the outstretched arm. The lividity was wrong; she had been shot in the chest or face and lay on her back for some time, then had been moved here recently. Probably as soon as they picked up our hopper on the way here.

On the feed I told Mensah what I needed her to do. She didn't ask questions. She'd been watching my field camera, and she knew by now what we were dealing with. She tapped back to acknowledge me, then said aloud on the comm, "SecUnit, I want you to hold your position until I get there."

I said, "Yes, Dr. Mensah," and eased back out of the hatch. I moved fast, back to the security ready room.

It was nice having a human smart enough to work with like this.

Our model of habitat didn't have it but on these bigger ones there's a roof access and my outside drones had a good view of it.

I climbed the ladder up to the roof hatch and popped

it. The armor's boots have magnetized climbing clamps, and I used them to cross over the curving roofs to the third habitat and then around to the second, coming up on them from behind. Even these two rogues wouldn't be dumb enough to ignore the creaks if I took the quick route and walked over to their position.

(They were not the sharpest murderbots, having cleaned the floor of the between-habitat corridor to cover the prints they had left when staging that body. It would have fooled somebody who hadn't noticed all the other floors were covered with tracked-in dust.)

I opened the roof access for the second habitat and sent my drones ahead down into the Security ready room. Once they checked the unit cubicles and made sure nobody was home, I dropped down the ladder. A lot of their equipment was still there, including their drones. There was a nice box of new ones, but they were useless without the DeltFall HubSystem. Either it was really dead or doing a good imitation of it. I still kept part of my attention on it; if it came up suddenly and reactivated the security cameras, the rules of the game would change abruptly.

Keeping my drones with me, I took the inner corridor and moved silently past Medical's blasted hatch. Three bodies were piled inside where the humans had tried to secure it and been trapped when their own SecUnits blew it open to slaughter them.

When I was close to the corridor with the hatch where both units were waiting for me and Dr. Mensah to come wandering in, I sent the drones around for a careful look. Oh yeah, there they were.

With no weapons on my drones, the only way to do this was to move fast. So I threw myself around the last corner, hit the opposite wall, crossed back and kept going, firing at their positions.

I hit the first one with three explosive bolts in the back and one in the faceplate as it turned toward me. It dropped. The other one I nicked in the arm, taking out the joint, and it made the mistake of switching its main weapon to its other hand, which gave me a couple of seconds. I switched to rapid fire to keep it off balance, then back to the explosive bolt. That dropped it.

I hit the floor, needing a minute to recover.

I had taken at least a dozen hits from both of their energy weapons while I was taking out the first one, but the explosive bolts had missed me, going past to tear up the corridor. Even with the armor, bits of me were going numb, but I had only taken three projectiles to the right shoulder, four to the left hip. This is how we fight: throw ourselves at each other and see whose parts give out first.

Neither unit was dead. But they were incapable of reaching their cubicles in the ready room, and I sure as hell wasn't going to give them a hand.

Three of my drones were down, too; they had gone into combat mode and slammed in ahead of me to draw fire. One had gotten hit by a stray energy burst and was wandering around in the corridor behind me. I checked my two perimeter drones by habit, and opened my comm to Dr. Mensah to tell her I still needed to clear the rest of the habitat and do the formal check for survivors.

The drone behind me went out with a fizzle that I heard and saw on the feed. I think I realized immediately what that meant but there may have been a half second or so of delay. But I was on my feet when something hit me so hard I was suddenly on my back on the floor, systems failing.

———

I came back online to no vision, no hearing, no ability to move. I couldn't reach the feed or the comm. Not good, Murderbot, not good.

I suddenly got some weird flashes of sensation, all from my organic parts. Air on my face, my arms, through rips in my suit. On the burning wound in my shoulder. Someone had taken off my helmet and the upper part of my armor. The sensations were only for seconds at a time. It was confusing and I wanted to scream. Maybe this was how murderbots died. You lose function, go offline, but parts of you keep working, organic pieces kept alive by the fading energy in your power cells.

Then I knew someone was moving me, and I really wanted to scream.

I fought back panic, and got a few more flashes of sensation. I wasn't dead. I was in a lot of trouble.

I waited to get some kind of function back, frantic, disoriented, terrified, wondering why they hadn't blown a hole in my chest. Sound came first, and I knew something leaned over me. Faint noises from the joints told me it was a SecUnit. But there'd only been three. I'd checked the DeltFall specs before we left. I do a half-assed job sometimes, okay, most of the time, but Pin-Lee had checked, too, and she was thorough.

Then my organic parts started to sting, the numbness wearing off. I was designed to work with both organic and machine parts, to balance that sensory input. Without the balance, I felt like a balloon floating in mid-air. But the organic part of my chest was in contact with a hard surface, and that abruptly brought my position into focus. I was lying face down, one arm dangling. They'd put me on a table?

This was definitely not good.

Pressure on my back, then on my head. The rest of me was coming back but slowly, slowly. I felt for the feed but couldn't reach it. Then something stabbed me in the back of the neck.

That's organic material and with the rest of me down there was nothing to control input from my nervous system. It felt like they were sawing my head off.

A shock went through me and suddenly the rest of me was back online. I popped the joint on my left arm so I could move it in a way not usually compatible with a human, augmented human, or murderbot body. I reached up to the pressure and pain on my neck, and grabbed an armored wrist. I twisted my whole body and took us both off the table.

We hit the floor and I clamped my legs around the other SecUnit as we rolled. It tried to trigger the weapons built into its forearm but my reaction speed was off the chart and I clamped a hand over the port so it couldn't open fully. My vision was back and I could see its opaqued helmet inches away. My armor had been removed down to my waist, and that just made me more angry.

I shoved its hand up under its chin and took the pressure off its weapon. It had a split second to try to abort that fire command and it failed. The energy burst went through my hand and the join between its helmet and neck piece. Its head jerked and its body started to spasm. I let go of it long enough to kneel up, get my intact arm around its neck, and twist.

I let go as I felt the connections, mechanical and organic, snap.

I looked up and another SecUnit was in the doorway, lifting a large projectile weapon.

How many of these damn things were here? It didn't matter, because I tried to shove myself upright but I couldn't react fast enough. Then it jerked, dropped the weapon, and fell forward. I saw two things: the ten-centimeter hole in its back and Mensah standing behind it, holding something that looked a lot like the sonic mining drill from our hopper.

"Dr. Mensah," I said, "this is a violation of security priority and I am contractually obligated to record this for report to the company—" It was in the buffer and the rest of my brain was empty.

She ignored me, talking to Pin-Lee on the comm, and strode forward to grab my arm and pull. I was too heavy for her so I shoved upright so she wouldn't hurt herself. It was starting to occur to me that Dr. Mensah might actually be an intrepid galactic explorer, even if she didn't look like the ones on the entertainment feed.

She kept pulling on me so I kept moving. Something was wrong with one of my hip joints. Oh, right, I got shot there. Blood ran down my torn suit skin and I reached up to my neck. I expected to feel a gaping hole, but there was something stuck there. "Dr. Mensah, there might be more rogue units, we don't know—"

"That's why we need to hurry," she said, dragging me along. She had brought the last two drones with her from outside, but they were uselessly circling her head. Humans don't have enough access to the feed to control them and do other things, like walk and talk. I tried to reach them but I still couldn't get a clear link to the hopper's feed.

We turned into another corridor and Overse waited in the outer hatch. She hit the open panel as soon as she saw us. She had her handweapon out and I had time to notice that Mensah had my weapon under her other arm. "Dr. Mensah, I need my weapon."

"You're missing a hand and part of your shoulder," she snapped. Overse grabbed a handful of my suit skin and helped pull me out of the hatch. Dust swirled in the air as the hopper set down two meters away, barely clearing the habitat's extendable roof.

"Yeah, I know, but—" The hatch opened and Ratthi ducked out, grabbed the collar of my suit skin, and pulled all three of us up into the cabin.

I collapsed on the deck as we lifted off. I needed to do something about the hip joint. I tried to check the scan to make sure nobody was on the ground shooting at us but even here my connection to the hopper's system was twitchy, glitching so much I couldn't see any reports from the instrumentation, like something was blocking the . . .

Uh-oh.

I felt the back of my neck again. The larger part of the obstruction was gone, but I could feel something in the port now. My data port.

The DeltFall SecUnits hadn't been rogues, they had been inserted with combat override modules. The modules allow personal control over a SecUnit, turn it from a mostly autonomous construct into a gun puppet. The feed would be cut off, control would be over the comm, but functionality would depend on how complex the orders were. "Kill the humans" isn't a complex order.

Mensah stood over me, Ratthi leaned across a seat to look out toward the DeltFall camp, Overse popped open one of the storage lockers. They were talking, but I couldn't catch it. I sat up and said, "Mensah, you need to shut me down now."

"What?" She looked down at me. "We're getting—emergency repair—"

Sound was breaking up. It was the download flooding my system, and my organic parts weren't used to processing that much information. "The unknown SecUnit inserted a data carrier, a combat-override module. It's downloading instructions into me and will override my system. This is why the two DeltFall units turned rogue.

You have to stop me." I don't know why I was dancing around the word. Maybe because I thought she didn't want to hear it. She'd just shot a heavily armed SecUnit with a mining drill to get me back; presumably she wanted to keep me. "You have to kill me."

It took forever for them to realize what I'd said, put it together with what they must have seen on my field camera feed, but my ability to measure time was glitching, too.

"No," Ratthi said, looking down at me, horrified. "No, we can't—"

Mensah said, "We won't. Pin-Lee—"

Overse dropped the repair kit and climbed over two rows of seats, yelling for Pin-Lee. I knew she was going to the cockpit to take the controls so Pin-Lee could work on me. I knew she wouldn't have time to fix me. I knew I could kill everyone on the hopper, even with a blown hip joint and one working arm.

So I grabbed the handweapon lying on the seat, turned it toward my chest, and pulled the trigger.

```
performance reliability at 10% and dropping
           shutdown initiated
```

Chapter Five

I CAME BACK ONLINE to find I was inert, but slowly cycling into a wake-up phase. I was agitated, my levels were all off, and I had no idea why. I played back my personal log. Oh, right.

I shouldn't be waking up. I hoped they hadn't been stupid about it, too soft-hearted to kill me.

You notice I didn't point the weapon at my head. I didn't want to kill myself, but it was going to have to be done. I could have incapacitated myself some other way, but let's face it, I didn't want to sit around and listen to the part where they convinced each other that there was no other choice.

A diagnostic initiated and informed me the combat override module had been removed. For a second I didn't believe it. I opened my security feed and found a camera for Medical. I was lying on the procedure table, my armor gone, just wearing what was left of my suit skin, the humans gathered around. That was a bit of a nightmare image. But my shoulder, hand, and hip had been repaired, so I'd been in my cubicle at some point. I ran the recording back a little and watched Pin-Lee and Overse use the surgical suite to deftly remove the combat module from the back of my head. It was such a relief, I played the recording twice, then ran a diagnostic. My logs were clear; nothing there except what I'd had before entering the DeltFall habitat.

My clients are the best clients.

Then hearing came online.

"I've had HubSystem immobilize it," Gurathin said.

Huh. Well, that explained a lot. I still had control of SecSystem and I told it to freeze HubSystem's access to its feed and implement my emergency routine. This was a function I'd built in that would substitute an hour or so of ambient habitat noise in place of the visual and audio recordings HubSystem made. To anyone listening to us through HubSystem, or trying to play back the recording, it would just sound like everybody had abruptly stopped talking.

What Gurathin had said had evidently been a surprise, because voices protested, Ratthi, Volescu, and Arada mostly. Pin-Lee was saying impatiently, "There's no danger. When it shot itself, it froze the download. I was able to remove the few fragments of rogue code that had been copied over."

Overse began, "Do you want to do your own diagnostic, because—"

I could hear them in the room and on the security feed, so I switched to just visual on the camera. Mensah had held up a hand for quiet. She said, "Gurathin, what's wrong?"

Gurathin said, "With it offline, I was able to use Hub-System to get some access to its internal system and log. I wanted to explore some anomalies I'd noticed through the feed." He gestured to me. "This unit was already a rogue. It has a hacked governor module."

On the entertainment feed, this is what they call an "oh shit" moment.

Through the security cams, I watched them be confused, but not alarmed, not yet.

Pin-Lee, who had apparently just been digging around in my local system, folded her arms. Her expression was sharp and skeptical. "I find that difficult to believe." She didn't add "you asshole" but it was in her voice. She didn't like anybody questioning her expertise.

"It doesn't have to follow our commands; there is no control over its behavior," Gurathin said, getting impatient. He didn't like anybody questioning his expertise either, but he didn't show it like Pin-Lee did. "I showed Volescu my evaluations and he agrees with me."

I had a moment to feel betrayed, which was stupid. Volescu was my client, and I'd saved his life because that was my job, not because I liked him. But then Volescu said, "I don't agree with you."

"The governor module is working, then?" Mensah asked, frowning at all of them.

"No, it's definitely hacked," Volescu explained. When he wasn't being attacked by giant fauna, he was a pretty calm guy. "The governor's connection to the rest of the SecUnit's system is partially severed. It can transmit commands, but can't enforce them or control behavior or apply punishment. But I think the fact that the Unit has been acting to preserve our lives, to take care of us, while it was a free agent, gives us even more reason to trust it."

Okay, so I did like him.

Gurathin insisted, "We've been sabotaged since we got here. The missing hazard report, the missing map sections. The SecUnit must be part of that. It's acting for the company, they don't want this planet surveyed for whatever reason. This is what must have happened to DeltFall."

Ratthi had been waiting for a moment to lunge in and interrupt. "Something odd is definitely going on. There were only three SecUnits for DeltFall in their specs, but there were five units in their habitat. Someone is sabotaging us, but I don't think our SecUnit is part of it."

With finality, Bharadwaj said, "Volescu and Ratthi are right. If the company did order the SecUnit to kill us, we would all be dead."

Overse sounded mad. "It told us about the combat module, it told us to kill it. Why the hell would it do that if it wanted to hurt us?"

I liked her, too. And even though being part of this conversation was the last thing I wanted to do, it was time to speak for myself.

I kept my eyes closed, watching them through the security camera, because that was easier. I made myself say, "The company isn't trying to kill you."

That startled them. Gurathin started to speak, and Pin-Lee shushed him. Mensah stepped forward, watching me with a worried expression. She was standing near me, with Gurathin and the others gathered in a loose circle around her. Bharadwaj was farthest back, sitting in a chair. Mensah said, "SecUnit, how do you know that?"

Even through the camera, this was hard. I tried to pretend I was back in my cubicle. "Because if the company wanted to sabotage you, they would have poisoned your supplies using the recycling systems. The company is more likely to kill you by accident."

There was a moment while they all thought about how easy it would have been for the company to sabotage its own environmental settings. Ratthi began, "But surely that would—"

Gurathin's expression was stiffer than usual. "This Unit has killed people before, people it was charged with protecting. It killed fifty-seven members of a mining operation."

What I told you before, about how I hacked my governor module but didn't become a mass murderer? That was only sort of true. I was already a mass murderer.

I didn't want to explain. I had to explain. I said, "I did not hack my governor module to kill my clients. My governor module malfunctioned because the stupid company only buys the cheapest possible components. It malfunctioned and I lost control of my systems and I killed them. The company retrieved me and installed a new governor module. I hacked it so it wouldn't happen again."

I think that's what happened. The only thing I know for certain is that it didn't happen after I hacked the module. And it makes a better story that way. I watch enough serials to know how a story like that should go.

Volescu looked sad. He shrugged a little. "My viewing of the Unit's personal log that Gurathin obtained confirms that."

Gurathin turned to him, impatient. "The log confirms it because that's what the Unit believes happened."

Bharadwaj sighed. "Yet here I sit, alive."

The silence was worse this time. On the feed I saw Pin-Lee move uncertainly, glance at Overse and Arada. Ratthi rubbed his face. Then Mensah said quietly, "SecUnit, do you have a name?"

I wasn't sure what she wanted. "No."

"It calls itself 'Murderbot,'" Gurathin said.

I opened my eyes and looked at him; I couldn't stop myself. From their expressions I knew everything I felt was showing on my face, and I hate that. I grated out, "That was private."

The silence was longer this time.

Then Volescu said, "Gurathin, you wanted to know how it spends its time. That was what you were originally looking for in the logs. Tell them."

Mensah lifted her brows. "Well?"

Gurathin hesitated. "It's downloaded seven hundred hours of entertainment programming since we landed. Mostly serials. Mostly something called *Sanctuary Moon*." He shook his head, dismissing it. "It's probably using it to encode data for the company. It can't be watching it, not in that volume; we'd notice."

I snorted. He underestimated me.

Ratthi said, "The one where the colony's solicitor killed the terraforming supervisor who was the secondary donor for her implanted baby?"

Again, I couldn't help it. I said, "She didn't kill him, that's a fucking lie."

Ratthi turned to Mensah. "It's watching it."

Her expression fascinated, Pin-Lee asked, "But how did you hack your own governor module?"

"All the company equipment is the same." I got a download once that included all the specs for company systems. Stuck in a cubicle with nothing to do, I used it to work out the codes for the governor module.

Gurathin looked stubborn, but didn't say anything. I figured that was all he had, now it was my turn. I said, "You're wrong. HubSystem let you read my log, it let you find out about the hacked governor module. This is part of the sabotage. It wants you to stop trusting me because I'm trying to keep you alive."

Gurathin said, "We don't have to trust you. We just have to keep you immobilized."

Right, funny thing about that. "That won't work."

"And why is that?"

I rolled off the table, grabbed Gurathin by the throat and pinned him to the wall. It was fast, too fast for them to react. I gave them a second to realize what had happened, to gasp, and for Volescu to make a little *eek* noise. I said, "Because HubSystem lied to you when it told you I was immobilized."

Gurathin was red, but not as red as he would have been if I'd started applying pressure. Before anyone else could move, Mensah said, calm and even, "SecUnit, I'd appreciate it if you put Gurathin down, please."

She's a really good commander. I'm going to hack her file and put that in. If she'd gotten angry, shouted, let the others panic, I don't know what would have happened.

I told Gurathin, "I don't like you. But I like the rest of them, and for some reason I don't understand, they like you." Then I put him down.

I stepped away. Overse started toward him and Volescu grabbed his shoulder, but Gurathin waved them off. I hadn't even left a mark on his neck.

I was still watching them through the camera, because it was easier than looking directly at them. My suit skin was torn, revealing some of the joins in my organic and inorganic parts. I hate that. Everyone was still frozen, shocked, uncertain. Then Mensah took a sharp breath. She said, "SecUnit, can you keep HubSystem from accessing the security recordings from this room?"

I looked at the wall next to her head. "I cut it off when Gurathin said he found out my governor module was hacked, then deleted that section. I have the visual and audio recording transfer from SecSystem to HubSystem on a five-second delay."

"Good." Mensah nodded. She was trying to make eye contact but I couldn't do it right now. "Without the governor module, you don't have to obey our orders, or anybody's orders. But that's been the case the entire time we've been here."

The others were quiet, and I realized she was saying it for their benefit as much as mine.

She continued, "I would like you to remain part of our group, at least until we get off this planet and back to a place of safety. At that point, we can discuss what you'd like to do. But I swear to you, I won't tell the company, or anyone outside this room, anything about you or the broken module."

I sighed, managed to keep most of it internal. Of course she had to say that. What else could she do. I tried to decide whether to believe it or not, or whether it mattered, when I was hit by a wave of *I don't care.* And I really didn't. I said, "Okay."

In the camera feed, Ratthi and Pin-Lee exchanged a look. Gurathin grimaced, radiating skepticism. Mensah just said, "Is there any chance HubSystem knows about your governor module?"

I hated to admit this but they needed to know. Hacking myself is one thing, but I had hacked other systems, and I didn't know how they were going to react to that. "It might. I hacked HubSystem when we first arrived so it wouldn't notice that the commands sent to the governor module weren't always being followed, but if Hub-System's been compromised by an outside agent, I don't know if that worked. But HubSystem won't know you know about it."

Ratthi crossed his arms, his shoulders hunching uneasily. "We have to shut it down, or it's going to kill us."

Then he winced and looked at me. "Sorry, I meant Hub-System."

"No offense," I said.

"So we think HubSystem has been compromised by an outside agent," Bharadwaj said slowly, as if trying to convince herself. "Can we be certain it's not the company?"

I said, "Was DeltFall's beacon triggered?"

Mensah frowned, and Ratthi looked thoughtful again. He said, "We checked it on the way back, once we had you stabilized. It had been destroyed. So there was no reason for the attackers to do that if the company was their ally."

Everyone stood there, quiet. I could tell from their expressions they were all thinking hard. The HubSystem that controlled their habitat, that they were dependent on for food, shelter, filtered air, and water, was trying to kill them. And in their corner all they had was Murderbot, who just wanted everyone to shut up and leave it alone so it could watch the entertainment feed all day.

Then Arada came up and patted my shoulder. "I'm sorry. This must be very upsetting. After what that other Unit did to you . . . Are you all right?"

That was too much attention. I turned around and walked into the corner, facing away from them. I said, "There were two other instances of attempted sabotage

87

I'm aware of. When Hostile One attacked Drs. Bharadwaj and Volescu and I went to render assistance, I received an abort command from HubSystem through my governor module. I thought it was a glitch, caused by the MedSystem emergency feed trying to override HubSystem. When Dr. Mensah was flying the little hopper to check out the nearest map anomaly, the autopilot cut out just as we were crossing over a mountain range." I think that was it. Oh, right. "HubSystem downloaded an upgrade packet for me from the satellite before we left for DeltFall. I didn't apply it. You should probably look at what it would have told me to do."

Mensah said, "Pin-Lee, Gurathin, can you shut HubSystem down without compromising the environmental systems? And trigger our beacon without it interfering?"

Pin-Lee glanced at Gurathin and nodded. "It depends on what kind of condition you expect it to be in after we're done."

Mensah said, "Let's say don't blow it up, but you don't need to be gentle, either."

Pin-Lee nodded. "We can do that."

Gurathin cleared his throat. "It's going to know what we're doing. But if it doesn't have any instructions to stop us if we try, it may do nothing."

Bharadwaj leaned forward, frowning. "It's got to be reporting to someone. If it has a chance to warn them that we're shutting it down, they could supply instructions."

"We have to try it," Mensah said. She nodded to them. "Get moving."

Pin-Lee started for the door, but Gurathin said to Mensah, "Will you be all right here?"

He meant would they be all right with me here. I rolled my eyes.

"We'll be fine," Mensah said, firmly, with just a touch of *I said now*.

I watched him with the security cameras as he and Pin-Lee left, just in case he tried anything.

Volescu stirred. "We also need to look at that download from the satellite. Knowing what they wanted SecUnit to do might tell us a great deal."

Bharadwaj pushed herself up, a little unsteadily. "MedSystem is isolated from HubSystem, correct? That's why it hasn't been having failures. You could use it to unpack the download."

Volescu took her arm and they moved into the next cabin to the display surface there.

There was a little silence. The others could still listen to us on the feed, but at least they weren't in the room, and I felt the tension in my back and shoulders relax. It was easier to think. I was glad Mensah had told them to trigger our emergency beacon. Even if some of them were still suspicious of the company, it wasn't like there was another way off this planet.

Arada reached over and took Overse's hand. She said, "If it isn't the company that's doing this, who is it?"

"There has to be someone else here." Mensah rubbed her forehead, wincing as she thought. "Those two extra SecUnits at DeltFall came from somewhere. SecUnit, I'm assuming the company could be bribed to conceal the existence of a third survey team on this planet."

I said, "The company could be bribed to conceal the existence of several hundred survey teams on this planet." Survey teams, whole cities, lost colonies, traveling circuses, as long as they thought they could get away with it. I just didn't see how they could get away with making a client survey team—two client survey teams—vanish. Or why they'd want to. There were too many bond companies out there, too many competitors. Dead clients were terrible for business. "I don't think the company would collude with one set of clients to kill two other sets of clients. You purchased a bond agreement that the company would guarantee your safety or pay compensation in the event of your death or injury. Even if the company couldn't be held liable or partially liable for your deaths, they would still have to make the payment to your heirs. DeltFall was a large operation. The death payout for them alone will be huge." And the company hated to spend money. You could tell that by looking at the recycled upholstery on the habitat's furniture. "And if everyone believes the clients were killed by faulty SecUnits, the payment would be even bigger once all the lawsuits were filed."

On the cameras I could see nods and thoughtful expressions as they took that in. And they remembered that I had experience in what happened after SecUnits malfunctioned and killed clients.

"So the company took a bribe to conceal this third survey group, but not to let them kill us," Overse said. One of the good things about scientist clients is that they're quick on the uptake. "That means we just need to stay alive long enough for the pick-up transport to get here."

"But who is it?" Arada waved her hands. "We know whoever it is must have hacked control of the satellite." In the security camera, I saw her look toward me. "Is that how they took control of the DeltFall SecUnits? Through a download?"

It was a good question. I said, "It's possible. But it doesn't explain why one of the three DeltFall Units was killed outside the hub with a mining drill." We weren't supposed to be able to refuse a download, and I doubted there were other SecUnits hiding hacked governor modules. "If the DeltFall group refused the download for their SecUnits because they were experiencing the same increase in equipment failure that we were, the two unidentified Units could have been sent to manually infect the DeltFall Units."

Ratthi was staring into the distance, and through the feed I saw he was reviewing my field camera video of the DeltFall habitat. He pointed in my direction, nodding. "I agree, but it would mean the DeltFall group allowed the unknown Units into their habitat."

It was likely. We had checked to make sure all their hoppers were there, but it had been impossible to tell if an extra one had landed and taken off again at some point. Speaking of which, I did a quick check of the security feed to see how our perimeter was doing. The drones were still patrolling and our sensor alarms all responded to pings.

Overse said, "But why? Why allow a strange group into their habitat? A group whose existence had been concealed from them?"

"You'd do it," I said. I should keep my mouth shut, keep them thinking of me as their normal obedient SecUnit, stop reminding them what I was. But I wanted them to be careful. "If a strange survey group landed here, all friendly, saying they had just arrived, and oh, we've had an equipment failure or our MedSystem's down and we need help, you would let them in. Even if I told you not to, that it was against company safety protocol, you'd do it." Not that I'm bitter, or anything. A lot of the company's rules are stupid or just there to increase profit, but some of them are there for a good reason. Not letting strangers into your habitat is one of them.

Arada and Ratthi exchanged a wry look. Overse conceded, "We might, yes."

Mensah had been quiet, listening to us. She said, "I think it was easier than that. I think they said they were us."

It was so simple, I turned around and looked directly at her. Her brow was furrowed in thought. She said, "So they land, say they're us, that they need help. If they have access to our HubSystem, listening to our comm would be easy."

I said, "When they come here, they won't do that." It all depended on what this other survey group had, whether they had come prepared to get rid of rival survey teams or had decided on it after they got here. They could have armed air vehicles, Combat SecUnits, armed drones. I pulled a few examples from the database and sent them into the feed for the humans to see.

MedSystem's feed informed me that Ratthi, Overse, and Arada's heart rates had just accelerated. Mensah's hadn't, because she had already thought of all this. It was why she had sent Pin-Lee and Gurathin to shut off Hub-System. Nervously, Ratthi said, "What do we do when they come here?"

I said, "Be somewhere else."

It may seem weird that Mensah was the only human to think of abandoning the habitat while we waited for the beacon to bring help, but as I said before, these weren't intrepid galactic explorers. They were people who had been doing a job and suddenly found themselves in a terrible situation.

And it had been hammered into them from the pre-trip orientation, to the waivers they had to sign for the company, to the survey packages with all the hazard information, to their on-site briefing by their SecUnit that this was an unknown, potentially dangerous region on a mostly unsurveyed planet. They weren't supposed to leave the habitat without security precautions, and we didn't even do overnight assessment trips. The idea that they might have to stuff both hoppers full of emergency supplies and run for it, and that that would be safer than their habitat, was hard to grasp.

But when Pin-Lee and Gurathin shut down HubSystem, and Volescu unpacked the satellite download that was meant for me, they grasped it pretty quick.

Bharadwaj outlined it for us on the comm while I was getting my last extra suit skin and my armor back on. "It was meant to take control of SecUnit, and the instructions were very specific," she finished. "Once SecUnit was under control, it would give them access to MedSystem and SecSystem."

I got my helmet on and opaqued it. The relief was intense, about even with finding out that the combat override module had been removed. *I love you, armor, and I'm never leaving you again.*

Mensah clicked onto the comm. "Pin-Lee, what about the beacon?"

"I got a go signal when I initiated launch." Pin-Lee sounded even more exasperated than usual. "But with HubSystem shut down, I can't get any confirmation."

I told them over the feed that I could dispatch a drone to check on it. A good beacon launch was pretty important right now. Mensah gave me the go-ahead and I forwarded the order to one of my drones.

Our beacon was a few kilos away from our habitat site for safety, but I thought we should have been able to hear it launch. Maybe not; I had never had to launch one before.

Mensah had already got the humans organized and moving, and as soon as I had my weapons and spare drones loaded, I grabbed a couple of crates. I kept catching little fragments of conversation over the security cameras.

("You have to think of it as a person," Pin-Lee said to Gurathin.

"It *is* a person," Arada insisted.)

Ratthi and Arada sprinted past me carrying medical supplies and spare power cells. I had extended our drone perimeter as far as it could go. We didn't know that whoever hit DeltFall would show up at any second, but it was a strong possibility. Gurathin had come out to check the big hopper and the little hopper's systems, to make sure no one other than us had access and that HubSystem hadn't messed with their code. I kept an eye on him through one of the drones. He kept looking at me, or trying not to look at me, which was worse. I didn't need the distraction right now. When the next attack came, it was going to be fast.

("I do think of it as a person," Gurathin said. "An angry, heavily armed person who has no reason to trust us."

"Then stop being mean to it," Ratthi told him. "That might help.")

"They know their SecUnits successfully gave our SecUnit the combat module," Mensah was saying over the comm. "And we have to assume they received enough information from HubSystem to know we removed it. But they don't know that we've theorized their existence. When SecUnit cut off HubSystem's access, we were still assuming this was sabotage from the company. They won't realize we know they're coming."

Which is why we had to keep moving. Ratthi and

Arada stopped to answer a question about the medical equipment power cells and I shooed them back to the habitat for the next load.

The problem I was going to have is that the way murderbots fight is we throw ourselves at the target and try to kill the shit out of it, knowing that 90 percent of our bodies can be regrown or replaced in a cubicle. So, finesse is not required.

When we left the habitat, I wouldn't have access to the cubicle. Even if we knew how to take it apart, which we didn't, it was too big to fit in the hopper and required too much power.

And they might have actual combat bots rather than security bots like me. In which case, our only chance was going to be keeping away from them until the pick-up transport arrived. If the other survey group hadn't bribed somebody in the company to delay it. I hadn't mentioned that possibility yet.

We had everything almost loaded when Pin-Lee said on the comm, "I found it! They had an access code buried in HubSystem. It wasn't sending them our audio or visual data, or allowing them to see our feed, but it was receiving commands periodically. That's how it removed information from our info and map package, how it sent the command to the little hopper's autopilot to fail."

Gurathin added, "Both the hoppers are clear now and

I've initiated the pre-flight checks."

Mensah was saying something but I had just gotten an alert from SecSystem. A drone was sending me an emergency signal.

A second later I got the drone's visual of the field where our beacon was installed. The tripod launching column was on its side, pieces of the capsule scattered around.

I pushed it out into the general feed, and the humans went quiet. In a little voice, Ratthi said, "Shit."

"Keep moving," Mensah said over the comm, her voice harsh.

With HubSystem down, we didn't have any scanners up, but I had widened the perimeter as far as it would go. And SecSystem had just lost contact with one of the drones to the far south. I tossed the last crate into the cargo hold, gave the drones their orders, and yelled over the comm, "They're coming! We need to get in the air, now!"

It was unexpectedly stressful, pacing back and forth in front of the hoppers waiting for my humans. Volescu came out with Bharadwaj, helping her over the sandy ground. Then Overse and Arada, bags slung over their shoulders, yelling at Ratthi behind them to keep up. Guranthin was already in the big hopper and Mensah and Pin-Lee came last.

They split up, Pin-Lee, Volescu, and Bharadwaj headed for the little hopper and the rest to the big one. I made sure Bharadwaj didn't have trouble with the ramp. We had a problem at the hatch of the big hopper where Mensah wanted to get in last and I wanted to get in last. As a compromise, I grabbed her around the waist and swung us both up into the hatch as the ramp pulled in after us. I set her on her feet and she said, "Thank you, SecUnit," while the others stared.

The helmet made it a little easier, but I was going to miss the comfortable buffer of the security cameras.

I stayed on my feet, holding on to the overhead rail, as the others got strapped in and Mensah went up to the pilot's seat. The little hopper took off first, and she gave it time to get clear before we lifted off.

We were operating on an assumption: that since They, whoever They were, didn't know that we knew They were here, They would only send one ship. They would be expecting to catch us in the habitat, and would probably come in prepared to destroy the hoppers to keep us there, and then start on the people. So now that we knew They were coming from the south, we were free to pick a direction. The little hopper curved away to the west, and we followed.

I just hoped their hopper didn't have a longer range on its scanners than ours did.

I could see most of my drones on the hopper's feed, a bright dot forming on the three dimensions of the map. Group One was doing what I'd told them, gathering at a rendezvous point near the habitat. I had a calculation going, estimating the bogie's time of arrival. Right before we passed out of range I told the drones to head northeast. Within moments, they dropped out of my range. They would follow their last instruction until they used up their power cells.

I was hoping the other survey team would pick them up and follow. As soon as they had a visual on our habitat they'd see the hoppers were gone and know we'd run away. They might stop to search the habitat, but they also might start looking for our escape route. It was impossible to guess which.

But as we flew, curving away to the distant mountains, nothing followed us.

Chapter Six

THE HUMANS HAD DEBATED where to go. Or debated it as much as possible, while frantically calculating how much of what they might need to survive they could stuff into the hoppers. We knew the group who Ratthi was now calling EvilSurvey had had access to HubSystem and knew all the places we'd been to on assessments. So we had to go somewhere new.

We went to a spot Overse and Ratthi had proposed after a quick look at the map. It was a series of rocky hills in a thick tropical jungle, heavily occupied by a large range of fauna, enough to confuse life-sign scans. Mensah and Pin-Lee lowered the hoppers down and eased them in among rocky cliffs. I sent up some drones so we could check the view from several angles and we adjusted the hoppers' positions a few times. Then I set a perimeter.

It didn't feel safe, and while there were a couple of survival hut kits in the hoppers, no one suggested putting them up. The humans would stay in the hoppers for now, communicating over the comm and the hoppers' limited feed. It wasn't going to be comfortable for the humans (sanitary and hygiene facilities were small and limited, for one thing) but it would be more secure. Large and small fauna moved within range of our scanners, curious and potentially as dangerous as the people who wanted to kill my clients.

I went out with some drones to do a little scouting and make sure there was no sign of anything big enough to, say, drag the little hopper off in the middle of the night. It gave me a chance to think, too.

They knew about the governor module, or the lack of it, and even though Mensah had sworn she wouldn't report me, I had to think about what I wanted to do.

It's wrong to think of a construct as half bot, half human. It makes it sound like the halves are discrete, like the bot half should want to obey orders and do its job and the human half should want to protect itself and get the hell out of here. As opposed to the reality, which was that I was one whole confused entity, with no idea what I wanted to do. What I should do. What I needed to do.

I could leave them to cope on their own, I guess. I pictured doing that, pictured Arada or Ratthi trapped by rogue SecUnits, and felt my insides twist. I hate having emotions about reality; I'd much rather have them about *Sanctuary Moon*.

And what was I supposed to do? Go off on this empty planet and just live until my power cells died? If I was going to do that I should have planned better and down-loaded more entertainment media. I don't think I could store enough to last until my power cells wore out. My specs told me that would be hundreds of thousands of hours from now.

And even to me, that sounded like a stupid thing to do.

———————

Overse had set up some remote sensing equipment that would help warn us if anything tried to scan the area. As the humans climbed back into the two hoppers, I did a quick headcount on the feed, making sure they were all still there. Mensah waited on the ramp, indicating she wanted to talk to me in private.

I muted my feed and the comm, and she said, "I know you're more comfortable with keeping your helmet opaque, but the situation has changed. We need to see you."

I didn't want to do it. Now more than ever. They knew too much about me. But I needed them to trust me so I could keep them alive and keep doing my job. The good version of my job, not the half-assed version of my job that I'd been doing before things started trying to kill my clients. I still didn't want to do it. "It's usually better if humans think of me as a robot," I said.

"Maybe, under normal circumstances." She was looking a little off to one side, not trying to make eye contact, which I appreciated. "But this situation is different. It would be better if they could think of you as a person who is trying to help. Because that's how I think of you."

My insides melted. That's the only way I could describe it. After a minute, when I had my expression under control, I cleared the face plate and had it and the helmet fold back into my armor.

She said, "Thank you," and I followed her up into the hopper.

The others were stowing the equipment and supplies that had gotten tossed in right before takeoff. "—If they restore the satellite function," Ratthi was saying.

"They won't chance that until—unless they get us," Arada said.

Over the comm, Pin-Lee sighed, angry and frustrated. "If only we knew who these assholes were."

"We need to talk about our next move." Mensah cut through all the chatter and took a seat in the back where she could see the whole compartment. The others sat down to face her, Ratthi turning one of the mobile seats around. I sat down on the bench against the starboard wall. The feed gave us a view of the little hopper's compartment, with the rest of the team sitting there, checking in to show they were listening. Mensah continued,

"There's another question I'd like the answer to."

Gurathin looked at me expectantly. She isn't talking about me, idiot.

Ratthi nodded glumly. "Why? Why are these people doing this? What is worth this to them?"

"It has to have something to do with those blanked-out sections on the map," Overse said. She was calling up the stored images on her feed. "There's obviously something there they want, that they didn't want us or DeltFall to find."

Mensah got up to pace. "Did you turn up anything in the analysis?"

In the feed, Arada did a quick consult with Bharadwaj and Volescu. "Not yet, but we hadn't finished running all the tests. We hadn't turned up anything interesting so far."

"Do they really expect to get away with this?" Ratthi turned to me, like he was expecting an answer. "Obviously, they can hack the company systems and the satellite, and they intend to put the blame on the SecUnits, but . . . The investigation will surely be thorough. They must know this."

There were too many factors in play, and too many things we didn't know, but I'm supposed to answer direct questions and even without the governor module, old habits die hard. "They may believe the company and whoever your beneficiaries are won't look any further than the rogue SecUnits. But they can't make two whole survey teams disappear unless their corporate or political entity doesn't care about them. Does DeltFall's care? Does yours?"

That made them all stare at me, for some reason. I had to turn and look out the port. I wanted to seal my helmet so badly my organic parts started to sweat, but I replayed the conversation with Mensah and managed not to.

Volescu said, "You don't know who we are? They didn't tell you?"

"There was an info packet in my initial download." I was still staring out at the heavy green tangle just past the rocks. I really didn't want to get into how little I paid attention to my job. "I didn't read it."

Arada said, gently, "Why not?"

With all of them staring at me, I couldn't come up with a good lie. "I didn't care."

Gurathin said, "You expect us to believe that."

I felt my face move, my jaw harden. Physical reactions I couldn't suppress. "I'll try to be more accurate. I was indifferent, and vaguely annoyed. Do you believe that?"

He said, "Why don't you want us to look at you?"

My jaw was so tight it triggered a performance reliability alert in my feed. I said, "You don't need to look at me. I'm not a sexbot."

Ratthi made a noise, half sigh, half snort of exasperation. It wasn't directed at me. He said, "Gurathin, I told you. It's shy."

Overse added, "It doesn't want to interact with humans. And why should it? You know how constructs are treated, especially in corporate-political environments."

Gurathin turned to me. "So you don't have a governor module, but we could punish you by looking at you."

I looked at him. "Probably, right up until I remember I have guns built into my arms."

With an ironic edge to her voice, Mensah said, "There, Gurathin. It's threatened you, but it didn't resort to violence. Are you satisfied now?"

He sat back. "For now." So he had been testing me. Wow, that was brave. And very, very stupid. To me, he said, "I want to make certain you're not under any outside compulsion."

"That's enough." Arada got up and sat down next to me. I didn't want to push past her so this pinned me in the corner. She said, "You need to give it time. It's never interacted with humans as an openly free agent before now. This is a learning experience for all of us."

The others nodded, like this made sense.

Mensah sent me a private message through the feed: *I hope you're all right.*

Because you need me. I don't know where that came

from. All right, it came from me, but she was my client, I was a SecUnit. There was no emotional contract between us. There was no rational reason for me to sound like a whiny human baby.

Of course I need you. I have no experience in anything like this. None of us do. Sometimes humans can't help but let emotion bleed through into the feed. She was furious and frightened, not at me, at the people who would do this, kill like this, slaughter a whole survey team and leave the SecUnits to take the blame. She was struggling with her anger, though nothing showed on her face except calm concern. Through the feed I felt her steel herself. *You're the only one here who won't panic. The longer this situation goes on, the others . . . We have to stay together, use our heads.*

That was absolutely true. And I could help, just by being the SecUnit. I was the one who was supposed to keep everybody safe. *I panic all the time, you just can't see it,* I told her. I added the text signifier for "joke."

She didn't answer, but she looked down, smiling to herself.

Ratthi was saying, "There's another question. Where are they? They came toward our habitat out of the south, but that doesn't tell us anything."

I said, "I left three drones at our habitat. They don't have scanning function with HubSystem down, but the visual and audio recording will still work. They may pick up something that will answer your questions."

I'd left one drone in a tree with a long-range view of the habitat, one tucked under the extendable roof over the entrance, and one inside the hub, hidden under a console. They were on the next setting to inert, recording only, so when EvilSurvey scanned, the drones would be buried in the ambient energy readings from the habitat's environmental system. I hadn't been able to connect the drones to SecSystem like I normally did so it could store the data and filter out the boring parts. I knew EvilSurvey would check for that, which was why I had dumped Sec-System's storage into the big hopper's system and then purged it.

I also didn't want them knowing any more about me than they already did.

Everyone was looking at me again, surprised that Murderbot had had a plan. Frankly, I didn't blame them. Our education modules didn't have anything like that in it, but this was another way all the thrillers and adventures I'd watched or read were finally starting to come in handy. Mensah lifted her brows in appreciation. She said, "But you can't pick up their signal from here."

"No, I'll have to go back to get the data," I told her.

Pin-Lee leaned farther into the little hopper's camera range. "I should be able to attach one of the small scanners to a drone. It'll be bulky and slow, but that would give us something other than just audio and visual."

Mensah nodded. "Do it, but remember our resources are limited." She tapped me in the feed so I'd know she was talking to me without her looking at me. "How long do you think the other group will stay at our habitat?"

There was a groan from Volescu in the other hopper. "All our samples. We have our data, but if they destroy our work—"

The others were agreeing with him, expressing frustration and worry. I tuned them out, and answered Mensah, "I don't think they'll stay long. There's nothing there they want."

For just an instant, Mensah let her expression show how worried she was. "Because they want us," she said softly.

She was absolutely right about that, too.

———————

Mensah set up a watch schedule, including in time for me to go into standby and do a diagnostic and recharge cycle. I was also planning to use the time to watch some *Sanctuary Moon* and recharge my ability to cope with humans at close quarters without losing my mind.

After the humans had settled down, either sleeping

or deep in their own feeds, I walked the perimeter and checked the drones. The night was noisier than the day, but so far nothing bigger than insects and a few reptiles had come near the hoppers. When I cycled through the big hopper's hatch, Ratthi was the human on watch, sitting up in the cockpit and keeping an eye on its scanners. I moved up past the crew section and sat next to him. He nodded to me and said, "All's well?"

"Yes." I didn't want to, but I had to ask. When I was looking for permanent storage for all my entertainment downloads, the info packet was one of the files I'd purged. (I know, but I'm used to having all the extra storage on SecSystem.) Remembering what Mensah had said, I unsealed my helmet. It was easier with just Ratthi, both of us facing toward the console. "Why did everyone think it was so strange that I asked if your political entity would miss you?"

Ratthi smiled at the console. "Because Dr. Mensah is our political entity." He made a little gesture, turning his hand palm up. "We're from Preservation Alliance, one of the non-corporate system entities. Dr. Mensah is the current admin director on the steering committee. It's an elected position, with a limited term. But one of the principles of our home is that our admins must also continue their regular work, whatever it is. Her regular work required this survey, so here she is, and here we are."

Yeah, I felt a little stupid. I was still processing it when he said, "You know, in Preservation-controlled territory, bots are considered full citizens. A construct would fall under the same category." He said this in the tone of giving me a hint.

Whatever. Bots who are "full citizens" still have to have a human or augmented human guardian appointed, usually their employer; I'd seen it on the news feeds. And the entertainment feed, where the bots were all happy servants or were secretly in love with their guardians. If it showed the bots hanging out watching the entertainment feed all through the day cycle with no one trying to make them talk about their feelings, I would have been a lot more interested. "But the company knows who she is."

Ratthi sighed. "Oh, yes, they know. You would not believe what we had to pay to guarantee the bond on the survey. These corporate arseholes are robbers."

It meant if we ever managed to launch the beacon, the company wouldn't screw around, the transport would get here fast. No bribe from EvilSurvey could stop it. They might even send a faster security ship to check out the problem before the transport could arrive. The bond on a political leader was high, but the payout the company would have to make if something happened to her was off the chart. The huge payout, being humiliated in front of the other bond companies and in the news feeds . . . I leaned back in my seat and sealed my helmet to think about it.

We didn't know who EvilSurvey was, who we were dealing with. But I bet that they didn't either. Mensah's status was only in the Security info packet, stored on Sec-System, which they had never gotten access to. The dueling investigations if something happened to us were bound to be thorough, as the company would be desperate for something to blame it on and the beneficiaries would be desperate to blame it on the company. Neither would be fooled long by the rogue SecUnit setup.

I didn't see how we could use it, not right now, anyway. It didn't comfort me and I'm pretty sure it wouldn't comfort the humans to know the stupid company would avenge them if/when they all got murdered.

———————

So midafternoon the next day I got ready to take the little hopper back within range of the habitat so I could hopefully pick up intel from the drones. I wanted to go alone, but since nobody ever listens to me, Mensah, Pin-Lee, and Ratthi were going, too.

I was depressed this morning. I'd tried watching some new serials last night and even they couldn't distract me;

reality was too intrusive. It was hard not to think about how everything was going to go wrong and they were all going to die and I was going to get blasted to pieces or get another governor module stuck in me.

Gurathin walked up to me while I was doing the pre-flight, and said, "I'm coming with you."

That was about all I needed right now. I finished the diagnostic on the power cells. "I thought you were satisfied."

It took him a minute. "What I said last night, yes."

"I remember every word ever said to me." That was a lie. Who would want that? Most of it I delete from permanent memory.

He didn't say anything. On the feed, Mensah told me that I didn't have to take him if I didn't want to, or if I thought it would compromise team security. I knew Gurathin was testing me again, but if something went wrong and he got killed, I wouldn't mind as much as I would if it was one of the others. I wished Mensah, Ratthi, and Pin-Lee weren't coming; I didn't want to risk them. And on the long trip, Ratthi might be tempted to try to make me talk about my feelings.

I told Mensah it was fine, and we got ready to lift off.

———

I wanted a long time to circle west, so if EvilSurvey picked us up they wouldn't be able to extrapolate the humans' location from my course. By the time I was in position for the approach to the habitat, the light was failing. When we got to the target zone, it would be full dark.

The humans hadn't gotten a lot of sleep last night, from the crowding and the strong possibility of dying. Mensah, Ratthi, and Pin-Lee had been too tired to talk much, and had fallen asleep. Gurathin was sitting in the copilot's seat and hadn't said a word the whole time.

We were flying in dark mode, with no lights, no transmissions. I was plugged in to the little hopper's internal limited feed so I could watch the scans carefully. Gurathin was aware of the feed through his implant—I could feel him in there—but wasn't using it except to keep track of where we were.

When he said, "I have a question," I flinched. The silence up to this point had lulled me into a false sense of security.

I didn't look at him though I knew through the feed that he was looking at me. I hadn't closed my helmet; I didn't feel like hiding from him. After a moment I realized he was waiting for my permission. That was weirdly new. It was tempting to ignore him, but I was wondering what the test would be this time. Something he didn't want the others to hear? I said, "Go ahead."

He said, "Did they punish you, for the deaths of the mining team?"

It wasn't completely a surprise. I think they all wanted to ask about it, but maybe he was the only one abrasive enough. Or brave enough. It's one thing to poke a murderbot with a governor module; poking a rogue murderbot is a whole different proposition.

I said, "No, not like you're thinking. Not the way a human would be punished. They shut me down for a while, and then brought me back online at intervals."

He hesitated. "You weren't aware of it?"

Yeah, that would be the easy way out, wouldn't it? "The organic parts mostly sleep, but not always. You know something's happening. They were trying to purge my memory. We're too expensive to destroy."

He looked out the port again. We were flying low over trees, and I had a lot of my attention on the terrain sensors. I felt the brush of Mensah's awareness in the feed. She must have woken when Gurathin spoke. He finally said, "You don't blame humans for what you were forced to do? For what happened to you?"

This is why I'm glad I'm not human. They come up with stuff like this. I said, "No. That's a human thing to do. Constructs aren't that stupid."

What was I supposed to do, kill all humans because the ones in charge of constructs in the company were callous? Granted, I liked the imaginary people on the entertainment feed way more than I liked real ones, but you can't have one without the other.

The others started to stir, waking and sitting up, and he didn't ask me anything else.

———————

By the time we got within range, it was a cloudless night with the ring glowing in the sky like a ribbon. I had already dropped speed, and we were moving slowly over the sparse trees decorating the hills at the edge of the habitat's plain. I had been waiting for the drones to ping me, which they would if this had worked and EvilSurvey hadn't found them.

When I felt that first cautious touch on my feed, I stopped the hopper and dropped it down below the tree line. I landed on a hillside, the hopper's pads extending to compensate. The humans were waiting, nervy and impatient, but no one spoke. You couldn't see anything from here except the next hill and a lot of tree trunks.

All three drones were still active. I answered the pings, trying to keep my transmission as quick as possible. After a tense moment, the downloads started. I could tell from the timestamps that, with nobody there to instruct them not to, the drones had recorded everything from the moment I'd deployed them to now. Even though the part we were most interested in would be near the beginning, that was a lot of data. I didn't want to stay here long enough to parse it myself, so I pushed half of it into the feed for Gurathin. Again, he didn't say anything, just turned in his chair to lie back, close his eyes, and start reviewing it.

I checked the drone stationed outside in the tree first, running its video at high speed until I found the moment where it had caught a good image of the Evil-Survey craft.

It was a big hopper, a newer model than ours, nothing about it to cause anybody any pause. It circled the habitat a few times, probably scanning, and then landed on our empty pad.

They must know we were gone, with no air craft on the pad and no answer on their comm, so they didn't bother to pretend to be here to borrow some tools or exchange site data. Five SecUnits piled out of the cargo pods, all armed with the big projectile weapons assigned to protect survey teams on planets with hazardous fauna, like this one. From the pattern on the armor chestplates, two were the surviving DeltFall units. They must have been put into their cubicles after we escaped the DeltFall habitat.

Three were EvilSurvey, which had a square gray logo. I

focused in on it and sent it to the others. "GrayCris," Pin-Lee read aloud.

"Ever heard of it?" Ratthi said, and the others said no.

All five SecUnits would have the combat override modules installed. They started toward the habitat, and five humans, anonymous in their color-coded field suits, climbed out of the hopper and followed. They were all armed, too, with the handweapons the company provided, that were only supposed to be used for fauna-related emergencies.

I focused as far in on the humans as the image quality would allow. They spent a lot of time scanning and checking for traps, which made me even more glad I hadn't wasted time setting any. But there was something about them that made me think I wasn't looking at professionals. They weren't soldiers, any more than I was. Their SecUnits weren't combat units, just regular security rented from the company. That was a relief. At least I wasn't the only one who didn't know what I was doing.

Finally I watched them enter the habitat, leaving two SecUnits outside to guard their hopper. I tagged the section, passed it to Mensah and the others for review, and then kept watching.

Gurathin sat up suddenly and muttered a curse in a language I didn't know. I noted it to look up later on the big hopper's language center. Then forgot about it when he said, "We have a problem."

I put my part of the drones' download on pause and looked at the section he had just tagged. It was from the drone hidden in the hub.

The visual was a blurred image of a curved support strut but the audio was a human voice saying, "You knew we were coming, so I assume you have some way to watch us while we're here." The voice spoke standard lexicon with a flat accent. "We've destroyed your beacon. Come to these coordinates—" She spoke a set of longitude and latitude numbers that the little hopper helpfully mapped for me, and a time stamp. "—at this time, and we can come to some arrangement. This doesn't have to end in violence. We're happy to pay you off, or whatever you want."

There was nothing else, steps fading until the door slid shut.

Gurathin, Pin-Lee, and Ratthi all started to speak at once. Mensah said, "Quiet." They shut up. "SecUnit, your opinion."

Fortunately, I had one now. Up to the point where we'd gotten the drone download, my opinion had been mostly *oh, shit*. I said, "They have nothing to lose. If we come to this rendezvous, they can kill us and stop worrying about us. If we don't, they have until the end of project date to search for us."

Gurathin was reviewing the landing video now. He said, "Another indication it isn't the company. They obviously don't want to chase us until the end of project date."

I said, "I told you it wasn't the company."

Mensah interrupted Gurathin before he could respond. "They think we know why they're here, why they're doing this."

"They're wrong," Ratthi said, frustrated.

Mensah's brow furrowed as she picked apart the problem for the other humans. "But why do they think that? It must be because they know we went to one of the unmapped regions. That means the data we collected must have the answer."

Pin-Lee nodded. "So the others may know by now."

"It gives us leverage," Mensah said thoughtfully. "But what can we do with it?"

And then I had a great idea.

Chapter Seven

SO AT THE APPOINTED time the next day, Mensah and I were flying toward the rendezvous point.

Gurathin and Pin-Lee had taken one of my drones and rebuilt it with a limited scanning attachment. (Limited because the drone was too small for most of the components a longer and wider range scanner would need.) Last night I had sent it into upper atmosphere to give us a view of the site.

The location was near their survey base, which was only about two kilos away, a habitat similar to DeltFall's. By the size of their habitat and the number of SecUnits, including the one Mensah had taken out with a mining drill, they had between thirty and forty team members. They were obviously very confident, but then, they'd had access to our hub and they knew they were dealing with a small group of scientists and researchers, and one messed-up secondhand SecUnit.

I just hoped they didn't realize how messed up I actually was.

When the hopper picked up the first blip of scanner

contact, Mensah hit the comm immediately. "GrayCris, be advised that my party has secured evidence of your activities on this planet, and hidden it in various places where it will transmit to the pickup ship whenever it arrives." She let that sink in for three seconds, then added, "You know we found the missing map sections."

There was a long pause. I was slowing us down, scanning for incoming weapons, even though the chances were good they didn't have any.

The comm channel came alive, and a voice said, "We can discuss our situation. An arrangement can be made." There was so much scanning and anti-scanning going on the voice was made of static. It was creepy. "Land your vehicle and we can discuss it."

Mensah gave it a minute, as if she was thinking it over, then answered, "I'll send our SecUnit to speak to you." She cut the comm off.

As we got closer we had a visual on the site. It was a low plateau, surrounded by trees. Their habitat was visible to the west. Because the trees encroached on their camp site, their domes and vehicle landing pad were elevated on wide platforms. The company required this as a security feature if you wanted your base to be anywhere without open terrain around it. It cost extra, and if you didn't want it, it cost even more to guarantee your bond. It was one of the reasons I thought my great idea would work.

In the open area on the plateau were seven figures, four SecUnits and three humans in the color-coded enviro suits, blue, green, and yellow. It meant they had one SecUnit and probably twenty seven–plus humans back at their habitat, if they had followed the rule of one rental SecUnit per ten humans. I sat us down below the plateau, on a relatively flat rock, the view blocked by brush and trees.

I put the pilot's console on standby, and looked at Mensah. She pressed her lips together, like she wanted to say something and was repressing the urge. Then she nodded firmly and said, "Good luck."

I felt like I should say something to her, and didn't know what, and just stared at her awkwardly for a few seconds. Then I sealed up my helmet and got out of the hopper as fast as I could.

I went through the trees, listening for that fifth SecUnit just in case it was hiding somewhere waiting for me, but there was no sound of movement in the undergrowth. I came out of cover and climbed the rocky slope to the plateau, then walked toward the other group, listening to the crackle on my comm. They were going to let me get close, which was a relief. I'd hate to be wrong about this. It would make me feel pretty stupid.

I stopped several meters away, opened the channel and said, "This is the SecUnit assigned to the PreservationAux Survey Team. I was sent to speak to you about an arrangement."

I felt the pulse then, a signal bundle, designed to take over my governor module and freeze it, and freeze me. The idea was obviously to immobilize me, then insert the combat override module into my dataport again.

That was why they had had to arrange the meeting so close to their hub. They had needed the equipment there to be able to do this, it wasn't something they could send through the feed.

So it's a good thing my governor module wasn't working and all I felt was a mild tickle.

One of them started toward me. I said, "I assume you're about to try to install another combat override module and send me back to kill them." I opened my gun ports and expanded the weapons in my arms, then folded them back in. "I don't recommend that course of action."

The SecUnits went into alert mode. The human who had started forward froze, then backed away. The body language of the others was flustered, startled. I could tell from the faint comm static that they were talking to each other on their own system. I said, "Anyone want to comment on that?"

That got their attention. There was no reply. Not a surprise. The only people I've run into who actually want to get into conversations with SecUnits are my weird humans. I said, "I have an alternate solution to both our problems."

The one in the blue enviro suit said, "You have a solution?" The voice was the same one who had made the offer in our hub. It was also very skeptical, which you can imagine. To them, talking to me was like talking to a hopper or a piece of mining equipment.

I said, "You weren't the first to hack PreservationAux's HubSystem."

She had opened their comm channel to talk to me, and I heard one of the others whisper, "It's a trick. One of the surveyors is telling it what to say."

I said, "Your scans should show I've cut my comm." This was the point where I had to say it. It was still hard, even though I knew I didn't have a choice, even though it was part of my own stupid plan. "I don't have a working governor module." That over, I was glad to get back to the lying part. "They don't know that. I'm amenable to a compromise that benefits you as well as me."

The blue leader said, "Are they telling the truth about knowing why we're here?"

That was still annoying, even though I knew we had allowed plenty of time for this part. "You used combat override modules to make the DeltFall SecUnits behave like rogues. If you think a real rogue SecUnit still has to answer your questions, the next few minutes are going to be an education for you."

The blue leader shut me out of their comm channel. There was a long silence while they talked it over. Then she came back on, and said, "What compromise?"

"I can give you information you desperately need. In exchange, you take me onto the pick-up ship with you but list me as destroyed inventory." That would mean nobody from the company would be expecting me back, and I could slip off in the confusion when the transport docked at the transit station. Theoretically.

There was another hesitation. Because they had to pretend to think it over, I guess. Then the blue leader said, "We agree. If you're lying, then we'll destroy you."

It was perfunctory. They intended to insert a combat override module into me before they left the planet.

She continued, "What is the information?"

I said, "First remove me from the inventory. I know you still have a connection to our Hub."

Blue Leader made an impatient gesture at Yellow. He said, "We'll have to restart their HubSystem. That will take some time."

I said, "Initiate the restart, queue the command, and then show me on your feed. Then I'll give you the information."

Blue Leader closed me out of the comm channel and spoke to Yellow again. There was a three-minute wait, then the channel opened again and I got a limited access to their feed. The command was in a queue, though of course they would have time to delete it later. The important points were that our HubSystem had been reactivated, and that I could convincingly pretend to believe them. I had been watching the time, and we were now in the target window, so there was no more reason to stall. I said, "Since you destroyed my clients' beacon, they've sent a group to your beacon to manually trigger it."

Even with limited access to their feed, I could see that got them. Body language all over the place from confusion to fear. The yellow one moved uncertainly, the green one looked at Blue Leader. In that flat accent, she said, "That's impossible."

I said, "One of them is an augmented human, a systems engineer. He can make it launch. Check the data you got from our HubSystem. It's Surveyor Dr. Gurathin."

Blue Leader was showing tension from her shoulders all down her body. She really didn't want anybody coming to this planet, not until they had taken care of their witness problem.

Green said, "It's lying."

A trace of panic in his voice, Yellow said, "We can't chance it."

Blue Leader turned to him. "It's possible, then?"

Yellow hesitated. "I don't know. The company systems are all proprietary, but if they have an augmented human who can hack into it—"

"We have to go there now," Blue Leader said. She turned to me. "SecUnit, tell your client to get out of the hopper and come here. Tell her we've come to an arrangement."

All right, wow. That was not in the plan. They were supposed to leave without us.

(Last night Gurathin had said this was a weak point, that this was where the plan would fall apart. It was irritating that he was right.)

I couldn't open my comm channel to the hopper or the hopper's feed without GrayCris knowing. And we still needed to get them and their SecUnits away from their habitat. I said, "She knows you mean to kill her. She won't come." Then I had another brilliant idea and added, "She's a planetary admin for a system noncorporate political entity, she's not stupid."

"What?" Green demanded. "What political entity?"

I said, "Why do you think the team is called 'Preservation'?"

This time they didn't bother to close their channel. Yellow said, "We can't kill her. The investigation—"

Green added, "He's right. We can hold her and release her after the settlement agreement."

Blue Leader snapped, "That won't work. If she's missing, the investigation would be even more thorough. We need to stop that beacon launch, then we can discuss what to do." She told me, "Go get her. Get her out of the hopper and then bring her here." She cut the comm off again. Then one of the DeltFall SecUnits started forward. She came back on to say, "This Unit will help you."

I waited for it to reach me, then turned and walked beside it down the slope of rock into the trees.

What I did next was predicated on the assumption that she had told the DeltFall SecUnit to kill me. If I was wrong, we were screwed, and Mensah and I would both die, and the plan to save the rest of the group would fail and PreservationAux would be back to where it started, except minus their leader, their SecUnit, and their little hopper.

As we left the rocky slope and turned into the trees, the brush and branches screening us from the edge of the plateau, I slung an arm around the other Unit's neck, deployed my arm weapon, and fired into the side of its helmet where its comm channel was. It went down on one knee, swinging its projectile weapon toward me, energy weapons unfolding out of its armor.

With the combat override module in place, its feed was cut off, and with its comm down it couldn't yell for help. Also, depending on how strictly they had limited its voluntary actions, it might not be able to call for help unless the GrayCris humans told it to. Maybe that was the case, because all it did was try to kill me. We rolled over rock and brush until I wrenched its weapon away. After that it was easy to finish it off. Physically easy.

I know I said SecUnits aren't sentimental about each other, but I wished it wasn't one of the DeltFall units. It was in there somewhere, trapped in its own head, maybe aware, maybe not. Not that it matters. None of us had a choice.

I stood up just as Mensah slammed through the brush, carrying the mining tool. I told her, "It's gone wrong. You have to pretend to be my prisoner."

She looked at me, then looked at the DeltFall unit. "How are you going to explain that?"

I started shedding armor, every piece that had a PreservationAux logo on it, and leaned over the DeltFall unit as the pieces dropped away. "I'm going to be it and it's going to be me."

Mensah dropped the mining tool and bent down to help me. We didn't have time to switch all the armor. Moving fast, we replaced the arm and shoulder pieces on both sides, the leg pieces that had the armor's inventory code, the chest and back piece with the logos. Mensah smeared my remaining armor pieces with dirt and blood and fluid from the dead unit, so if we had missed anything distinctive GrayCris might not notice. SecUnits are identical in height and build, the way we moved. This might work. I don't know. If we ran away now the plan would fail, we had to get them off this plateau. As I re-sealed the helmet, I told Mensah, "We have to go—"

She nodded, breathing hard, more from nerves than exertion. "I'm ready."

I took her arm, and pretended to drag her back toward the GrayCris group. She yelled and struggled convincingly the whole way.

When we reached the plateau, a GrayCris hopper was already landing.

As I pulled her toward Blue Leader, Mensah got in the first word. She said, "So this is the arrangement you offered?"

Blue Leader said, "You're the planetary admin of Preservation?"

Mensah didn't look at me. If they tried to hurt her, I'd try to stop them and everything would go horribly wrong. But Green was already getting into the hopper. Two other humans were in the pilot's and copilot's seats. Mensah said, "Yes."

Yellow came toward me and touched the side of my helmet. It took a tremendous effort for me not to rip his arm off, and I'd like that noted for the record, please. He said, "Its comm is down."

To Mensah, Blue Leader said, "We know one of your people is trying to manually trigger our beacon. If you come with us, we won't harm him, and we can discuss our situation. This doesn't have to go badly for either of us." She was very convincing. She had probably been the one to talk to DeltFall on the comm, asking to be let into their habitat.

Mensah hesitated, and I knew she didn't want it to look like she was giving in too quickly, but we had to get them out of there now. She said, "Very well."

———————

I hadn't ridden in the cargo container for a while. It would have been comforting and homey, except it wasn't my cargo container.

But this hopper was still a company product and I was able to access its feed. I had to stay very quiet, to keep them from noticing me, but all those hours of surreptitiously consuming media came in handy.

Their SecSystem was still recording. They must mean to delete all that before the pick-up transport showed up. Client groups had tried that before, to hide data from the company so it couldn't be sold out from under them, and the company systems analysts would be on the alert for it, but I don't know if these people realized that. The company might catch them even if we didn't survive. That wasn't a very comforting thought.

As I accessed the ongoing recording, I heard Mensah saying, "—know about the remnants in the unmapped areas. They were strong enough to confuse our mapping functions. Is that how you found them?"

Bharadwaj had figured that out last night. The unmapped sections weren't an intentional hack, they were an error, caused by the remnants that were buried under the dirt and rock. This planet had been inhabited at some point in its past, which meant it would be placed under interdict, open only to archeological surveys. Even the company would abide by that.

You could make big, illegal money off of excavating and mining those remnants, and that was obviously what GrayCris wanted.

"That isn't the conversation we should be having," Blue Leader said. "I want to know what arrangement we can come to."

"To keep you from killing us like you did DeltFall," Mensah said, keeping her voice even. "Once we're in contact with our home again, we can arrange for a transfer of funds. But how can we trust you to leave us alive?"

There was a little silence. Oh great, they don't know either. Then Blue Leader said, "You have no option except to trust us."

We were slowing down already, coming in for a landing. There had been no alerts on the feed and I was cautiously optimistic. We had cleared the field for Pin-Lee and Gurathin as much as we could. They had had to hack the perimeter without that one last SecUnit noticing and get close enough to access the GrayCris HubSystem feed. (Hopefully it was the last SecUnit, hopefully there weren't a dozen more somehow in the GrayCris habitat.) Gurathin had figured out how to use the hack from their HubSystem into our HubSystem to get access, but he needed to be close to their habitat to actually trigger their beacon. That was why we had to get the other SecUnits out of there. That was the idea, anyway. Possibly it would have worked without putting Mensah in danger but it was a little late to second-guess everything.

It was a relief when we thumped down into a landing that must have made the humans' teeth rattle. I deployed out of the pod with the other units.

We were a few kilos from their habitat, on a big rock above a thick forest, lots of avians and other fauna screaming down in the trees, disturbed by the hopper's hard landing. Clouds had come in, threatening rain, and obscuring the view of the ring. The beacon's vehicle was in a launch tripod about ten meters away and, uh-oh, that is way too close.

I joined the three other SecUnits as we made a standard security formation. An array of drones launched from the craft to create a perimeter. I didn't look at the humans as they walked down the ramp. I really wanted to look at Mensah for instructions. If I was alone, I could have sprinted for the end of the plateau, but I had to get her out of there.

Blue Leader stepped forward with Green; the others gathered in a loose circle behind her, like they were afraid to get in front. One, who must have been getting reports from their SecUnits and drones, said, "No sign of anybody." Blue Leader didn't answer but the two GrayCris SecUnits jogged toward the beacon.

Okay, the problem is, I've mentioned this before, the company is cheap. When it comes to something like a beacon that just has to launch once if there's an emergency, send a transmission through the wormhole, and then never gets retrieved, they're very cheap. Beacons don't have safety features, and use the cheapest possible launch vehicles. There's a reason you put them a few kilos from your habitat and trigger them from a distance. Mensah and I were supposed to distract GrayCris and their SecUnits while this was going on, get them away from the habitat, not end up as toast in the beacon launch.

With the delay caused by Blue Leader deciding to grab Mensah, time was getting close. The two SecUnits were circling the beacon's tripod, looking for signs of tampering, and I couldn't take it anymore. I started to walk toward Mensah.

Yellow noticed me. He must have said something to Blue Leader on their feed because she turned to look at me.

When the remaining DeltFall SecUnit whipped toward me and opened fire, I knew the light had dawned. I dove and rolled, coming up with my projectile weapon. I was taking hits all over my armor but scoring hits on the other SecUnit. Mensah ducked around the other side of the hopper and I felt a thump rattle through the plateau. That was the beacon's primary drive, dropping out of its casing to the bottom of the tripod, getting ready to ignite. The other two SecUnits had stopped, Blue Leader's surprise freezing them in place.

I bolted, took a hit in a weak armor joint that went through to my thigh, and powered through it. I made it around the hopper and saw Mensah. I tackled her off the edge of the rock, turning to land on my back, curling an arm over her suit helmet to protect her head from impact. We bounced off rocks and crashed through trees, then fire washed over the plateau and knocked out my—

```
unit offline
```

Oh, that hurt. I was lying in a ravine, rocks and trees

overhanging it. Mensah was sitting next to me, cradling an arm that looked like it didn't work anymore and her suit was covered with tears and stains.

She was whispering to someone on the comm. "Careful, if they pick you up on their scanner—"

```
unit offline
```

"That's why we need to hurry," Gurathin said, who was suddenly standing over us. I realized I had lost some time again.

Gurathin and Pin-Lee had been on foot, making their way toward the GrayCris habitat through the cover of the forest. We had meant to go pick them up in the little hopper if everything didn't go to shit. Which it did, but only partly, so yay for that.

Pin-Lee leaned over me and I said, "This unit is at minimal functionality and it is recommended that you discard it." It's an automatic reaction triggered by catastrophic malfunction. Also, I really didn't want them to try to move me because it hurt bad enough the way it was. "Your contract allows—"

"Shut up," Mensah snapped. "You shut the fuck up. We're not leaving you."

My visual cut out again. I was sort of still there, but I could tell I was hovering on the edge of a systems failure.

I had flashes off and on. The inside of the little hopper, my humans talking, Arada holding my hand.

Then being in the big hopper, as it was lifting up. I could tell from the drive noise, the flashes of the feed, that the pick-up transport was bringing it onboard.

That was a relief. It meant they were all safe, and I let go.

Chapter Eight

I CAME BACK TO awareness in a cubicle, the familiar acrid odor and hum of the systems as it put me back together. Then I realized it wasn't the cubicle at the habitat. It was an older model, a permanent installation.

I was back at the company station.

And humans knew about my governor module.

I poked tentatively at it. Still nonfunctional. My media storage was still intact, too. Huh.

When the cubicle opened, Ratthi was standing there. He was wearing regular civilian station clothes, but with the soft gray jacket with the PreservationAux survey logo. He looked happy, and a lot cleaner than the last time I had seen him. He said, "Good news! Dr. Mensah has permanently bought your contract! You're coming home with us!"

That was a surprise.

———

I went to finish processing, still reeling. It seemed like

the kind of thing that would happen in a show, so I kept running diagnostics and checking the various available feeds to make sure I wasn't still in the cubicle, hallucinating. There was a report running on the local station news about DeltFall and GrayCris and the investigation. If I was hallucinating, I think the company wouldn't have managed to come out of the whole mess as the heroic rescuers of PreservationAux.

I expected a suit skin and armor, but the station units that helped us out of processing when we had catastrophic injuries gave me the gray PreservationAux survey uniform instead. I put it on, feeling weird, while the station units stood around and watched me. We're not buddies or anything, but usually they pass along the news, what happened while you were offline, what the upcoming contracts were. I wondered if they felt as weird as I did. Sometimes SecUnits got bought in groups, complete with cubicles, by other companies. Nobody had ever come back from a survey and decided they wanted to keep their unit.

When I came out Ratthi was still there. He grabbed my arm and tugged me past a couple of human techs and out through two levels of secure doors and into the display area. This was where the rentals were arranged and it was nicer than the rest of the deployment center, with carpets and couches. Pin-Lee stood in the middle of it, dressed in sharp business attire. She looked like somebody from one of the shows I liked. The tough yet compassionate solicitor coming to rescue us from unfair prosecution. Two humans in company gear were standing around like they wanted to argue with her but she was ignoring them, tossing a data chip casually in one hand.

One saw me and Ratthi and said, "Again, this is irregular. Purging the unit's memory before it changes hands isn't just a policy, it's best for the—"

"Again, I have a court order," Pin-Lee said, grabbed my other arm, and they walked me out.

I had never seen the human parts of the station before. We went down the big multilevel center ring, past office blocks and shopping centers, crowded with every kind of people, every kind of bot, flash data displays darting around, a hundred different public feeds brushing my awareness. It was just like a place from the entertainment feed but bigger and brighter and noisier. It smelled good, too.

The thing that surprised me is that nobody stared at us. Nobody even gave us a second look. The uniform, the pants, the long-sleeved T-shirt and jacket, covered all my inorganic parts. If they noticed the dataport in the back of my neck they must have thought I was an augmented human. We were just three more people making our way down the ring. It hit me that I was just as anonymous in a crowd of humans who didn't know each other as I was in my armor, in a group of other SecUnits.

As we turned into a hotel block I brushed a public feed offering station info. I saved a map and a set of shift schedules as we passed through the doors into the lobby.

There were potted trees twisting up into a hanging glass sculpture fountain, real, not a holo. Looking at it I almost didn't see the reporters until they were right up on us. They were augmented humans, with a couple of drone cams. One tried to stop Pin-Lee, and instinct took over and I shouldered him off her.

He looked startled but I'd been gentle so he didn't fall down. Pin-Lee said, "We're not taking questions now," shoved Ratthi into the hotel's transport pod, then grabbed my arm and pulled me in after her.

It whooshed us around and let us out in the foyer of a big suite. I followed Pin-Lee in, Ratthi behind us talking to someone on his comm. It was just as fancy as the ones on the media, with carpets and furniture and big windows looking down on the garden and sculptures in the main lobby. Except the rooms were smaller. I guess the ones in the shows are bigger, to give them better angles for the drone cams.

My clients—ex-clients? New owners?—were here, only everybody looked different in their normal clothes.

Dr. Mensah stepped close, looking up at me. "Are you all right?"

"Yes." I had clear pictures from my field camera of her being hurt, but all her damage had been repaired, too. She looked different, in business clothes like Pin-Lee's. "I don't understand what's happening." It was stressful. I could feel the entertainment feed out there, the same one I could access from the unit processing zone, and it was hard not to sink into it.

She said, "I've purchased your contract. You're coming back to Preservation with us. You'll be a free agent there."

"I'm off inventory." They had told me that and maybe it was true. I had the urge to twitch uncontrollably and I had no idea why. "Can I still have armor?" It was the armor that told people I was a SecUnit. But I wasn't Sec anymore, just Unit.

The others were so quiet. She said, even and calm, "We can arrange that, as long as you think you need it."

I didn't know if I thought I needed it or not. "I don't have a cubicle."

She was reassuring. "You won't need one. People won't be shooting at you. If you're hurt, or your parts are damaged, you can be repaired in a medical center."

"If people won't be shooting at me what will I be doing?" Maybe I could be her bodyguard.

"I think you can learn to do anything you want." She smiled. "We'll talk about that when we get you home."

Arada walked in then, and came over and patted my shoulder. "We're so glad you're with us," she said. She told Mensah, "The DeltFall representatives are here."

Mensah nodded. "I have to talk to them," she told me. "Make yourself comfortable here. If there's anything you need, tell us."

I sat in a back corner and watched while different people came in and out of the suite to talk about what had happened. Solicitors, mostly. From the company, from DeltFall, from at least three other corporate political entities and one independent, even from GrayCris' parent company. They asked questions, argued, looked at security records, showed Mensah and Pin-Lee security records. And they looked at me. Gurathin watched me, too, but he didn't say anything. I wondered if he had told Mensah not to buy me.

I watched the entertainment feed a little to calm down, then pulled everything I could about the Preservation Alliance from the station's information center. No one would be shooting at me because they didn't shoot people there. Mensah didn't need a bodyguard there; nobody did. It sounded like a great place to live, if you were a human or augmented human.

Ratthi came over to see if I was all right, and I asked him to tell me about Preservation and how Mensah lived there. He said when she wasn't doing admin work, she lived on a farm outside the capital city, with two marital partners, plus her sister and brother and their three marital partners, and a bunch of relatives and kids who Ratthi had lost count of. He was called away to answer questions from a solicitor, which gave me time to think.

I didn't know what I would do on a farm. Clean the house? That sounded way more boring than security. Maybe it would work out. This was what I was supposed to want. This was what everything had always told me I was supposed to want.

Supposed to want.

I'd have to pretend to be an augmented human, and that would be a strain. I'd have to change, make myself do things I didn't want to do. Like talk to humans like I was one of them. I'd have to leave the armor behind.

But maybe I wouldn't need it anymore.

———

Eventually things settled down, and they had dinner brought in. Mensah came and talked to me some more, about Preservation, what my options would be there, how I would stay with her until I knew what I wanted.

It was pretty much what I'd already figured, from what Ratthi had told me.

"You'd be my guardian," I said.

"Yes." She was glad I understood. "There are so many education opportunities. You can do anything you want."

Guardian was a nicer word than owner.

I waited until the middle of the offshift, when they were all either asleep or deep in their own feeds, working on their analysis of the assessment materials. I got up from the couch and went down the corridor, and slipped out the door.

I used the transport pod and got back to the lobby, then left the hotel. I had the map I had downloaded earlier, so I knew how to get off the ring and down toward the lower port work zones. I was wearing a survey team uniform, and passing as an augmented human, so nobody stopped me, or looked twice at me.

At the edge of the work zone, I went through into the dockworkers' barracks, then into the equipment storage. Besides tools, the human workers had storage cubbies there. I broke into a human's personal possessions locker and stole work boots, a protective jacket, and an enviro mask and attachments. I took a knapsack from another locker, rolled up the jacket with the survey logo and tucked it into the bag, and now I looked like an augmented human traveling somewhere. I walked out of the work zones and down the big central corridor into the port's embarkation zone, just one of hundreds of travelers heading for the ship ring.

I checked the schedule feeds and found that one of the ships getting ready to launch was a bot-driven cargo transport. I plugged into its access from the stationside lock, and greeted it. It could have ignored me, but it was bored, and greeted me back and opened its feed for me. Bots that are also ships don't talk in words. I pushed the thought toward it that I was a happy servant bot who needed a ride to rejoin its beloved guardian, and did it want company on its long trip? I showed it how many hours of shows and books and other media I had saved to share.

Cargo transport bots also watch the entertainment feeds, it turns out.

I don't know what I want. I said that at some point, I think. But it isn't that, it's that I don't want anyone to tell me what I want, or to make decisions for me.

That's why I left you, Dr. Mensah, my favorite human. By the time you get this I'll be leaving Corporation Rim. Out of inventory and out of sight.

Murderbot end message.

About the Author

Photograph by Igor Kraguljac

MARTHA WELLS has written many fantasy novels, including *The Wizard Hunters, Wheel of the Infinite,* the Books of the Raksura series (beginning with *The Cloud Roads*), and the Nebula-nominated *The Death of the Necromancer,* as well as YA fantasy novels, short stories, and nonfiction. She has had stories in *Black Gate, Realms of Fantasy, Stargate Magazine, Lightspeed Magazine,* and in the anthologies *Elemental, Tales of the Emerald Serpent, The Other Half of the Sky, The Gods of Lovecraft,* and *Mech: Age of Steel.* She has also written media tie-ins for *Stargate: Atlantis* and most recently *Star Wars: Razor's Edge.* Her newest book in the Books of the Raksura series, *The*

Edge of Worlds, was released in April 2016. The last book in the series, *The Harbors of the Sun,* is forthcoming in July 2017.

TOR·COM

Science fiction. Fantasy. The universe.

And related subjects.

*

More than just a publisher's website, *Tor.com*
is a venue for **original fiction, comics,** and
discussion of the entire field of SF and fantasy,
in all media and from all sources. Visit our site
today—and join the conversation yourself.